AN ADAPTED CLASSIC

All Quiet on the Western Front

Erich Maria Remarque

GLOBE FEARON

Pearson Learning Group

Adapter: Tony Napoli
Project Editor: Kristen Shepos-Salvatore
Editorial Supervisor: Sandra Widener
Editorial Assistant: Kathleen Kennedy
Production Editor: Alan Dalgleish
Marketing Manager: Sandra Hutchison
Art Supervision: Patricia Smythe
Electronic Page Production: Luc Van Meerbeek
Cover and Interior Illustrator: James McDaniel

ISBN 0-8359-1869-6
Printed in the United States of America

12 13 14 15 V313 14 13 12 11

Globe Fearon

Pearson Learning Group

1-800-321-3106
www.pearsonlearning.com

CONTENTS

About the Author iv

Adapter's Note................................. v

Preface v

Historical Background vi

Author's Original Introduction viii

Chapter 1 1

Chapter 2 7

Chapter 3 13

Chapter 4 17

Chapter 5 26

Chapter 6 34

Chapter 7 44

Chapter 8 60

Chapter 9 64

Chapter 10 75

Chapter 11 86

Chapter 12 93

Reviewing Your Reading 95

ABOUT THE AUTHOR

Erich Maria Remarque was born in Osnabrück in Westphalia, Germany, in 1898. His father was German. His mother was of French descent. After completing his elementary school education, Remarque enrolled at the University of Münster. While attending the university, he was drafted into the German army. He was 18 years old.

During World War I, Remarque fought along the Western front. He was wounded five times, the last time seriously. After his discharge from the army, he worked at a number of different jobs. He was a teacher, a salesman for a tombstone firm, and an advertising writer for a tire company. This last job spurred his interest in auto racing and auto mechanics. It also led him to the beginning of his literary career.

He began by writing articles for a Swiss automobile magazine. Then he served as an assistant editor of the publication *Sportsbild.* In 1928, his first novel, *All Quiet on the Western Front,* was published. The book became an immediate and overwhelming success. It sold more than 1.5 million copies during the first year. It was later translated and published in 25 languages.

When the Nazis first came to power in Germany in the early 1930s, Remarque went to live in Switzerland. He did not return to Germany, and he began to write critically of the Nazi party. Because of this, his books were burned and banned. In 1938 his German citizenship was taken away.

In 1939, Remarque visited the United States. Eight years later, he became an American citizen. He spent his years in New York and in California, where he wrote several screenplays for Hollywood movies. Though he never again enjoyed the literary success of his first book, Remarque continued to write novels. His most successful other books were *Arch of Triumph* (1946), *The Black Obelisk* (1957), and *Heaven Has No Favorites* (1961). Erich Maria Remarque died in 1970.

ADAPTER'S NOTE

In preparing this edition of *All Quiet on the Western Front,* we have kept closely to what Erich Maria Remarque wrote. We have modified some vocabulary words and shortened and simplified many sentences and paragraphs. However, none of the story has been omitted.

PREFACE

All *Quiet on the Western Front* is the story of seven young German classmates who represent a generation changed forever by World War I, which is also known as the Great War. The novel is narrated by an idealistic young man named Paul Baümer. Because Remarque himself served in the war, the novel has always been considered a chilling first-hand account of how it feels to be caught up in the madness of war.

The novel is a huge success. It has sold millions of copies over the years and has been made into two very successful motion pictures. Still, when it was first published, it was very controversial in Germany.

Some people complained that it was filled with "weak pacifist" sentiments. Others charged that it was really "romantic propaganda for war." Remarque refused to take part in the debate. In the years since its publication, the novel continues to be thought of as the definitive statement against war.

HISTORICAL BACKGROUND

The Great War, as World War I was called, began in the summer of 1914. By the time it ended in the fall of 1918, more than 8 million men and women had died, and more than 20 million had been wounded. In the aftermath of the war, old empires crumbled, new countries were born, and an entire generation of young men was scarred forever.

In the early part of the 20th century, the countries of Europe had formed alliances or "friendships" among themselves. These alliances called for one country to come to the aid of another should that country find itself threatened. The major countries that formed these alliances had spent decades building up their armies and supply of weapons. So, by 1914, Europe was divided, more or less, into two armed camps: Germany and the empire of Austria-Hungary on one side; and Russia, France, Italy, and Great Britain on the other. Smaller countries such as Greece, Turkey, Serbia, Bulgaria, Romania, and Montenegro were also part of these alliances.

The act that triggered the war was an assassination. On June 28, 1914, the heir to the throne of the empire of Austria-Hungary, Archduke Francis Ferdinand, was murdered. He had been on a visit to the city of Sarajevo, the capital of Bosnia. While riding in a car with his wife, he was shot and killed by a 19-year-old terrorist from the neighboring country of Serbia. The assassin told police that he wanted to "avenge the Serbs for the oppression they had been suffering." There was no direct evidence that linked the young man to the Serbian government. Still, Austria-Hungary and its chief ally, Germany, reacted to the death by accusing the Serbian government of murder.

A month after the assassination, Austria-Hungary declared war on Serbia. Two days later, Serbia's main ally, Russia, mobilized its army. On August 1, Germany and Russia went to war. Germany fully expected that France, as Russia's ally, would enter the war. On August 2, the German army marched into Belgium, France's neighbor, and headed for Paris. This in turn brought Great Britain, a member of the Russia-France alliance, into the conflict. Germany and its allies became known as the Central Powers because of their location in Europe. The rest of Europe and Russia became known as the Allies.

For three years, the battles raged. Much of the heaviest fighting took place in France along the "Western Front." In 1917, the United States entered the war on the side of the Allies. Later that year, Russia's czar was overthrown and the new communist government pulled Russia out of the war.

America's support tipped the balance in the favor of the Allies. In 1918, one by one, the members of the Central Powers appealed for peace. First, the Austrian-Hungarian empire fell, and its emperor Charles I agreed to an armistice. The Hungarians,

Czechs, Slovaks, and Poles declared their independence. Inside Germany, the people were hungry and tired of the war. The German army was exhausted, and the troops were suffering heavy losses as they fell farther and farther into retreat. Finally, on November 11, an armistice was signed. Germany surrendered unconditionally, and the German leader, Kaiser Wilhelm, was forced to give up power. The most horrible war in history had finally come to an end.

AUTHOR'S ORIGINAL INTRODUCTION

This book is to be neither an accusation nor a confession, and least of all an adventure. For death is not an adventure to those who stand face to face with it. It will try simply to tell of a generation of men who, even though they may have escaped the shells, were destroyed by the war.

Chapter 1

We are at rest five miles behind the front lines and our bellies are full of food. Each man has another mess-tin full for the evening. What is more, there is a double ration of sausage and bread. We have not had such luck as this for a long time.

We have only a mistake to thank for it. Two weeks ago we had to go up and relieve the front line. It was fairly quiet in our sector. Headquarters ordered the usual amount of rations—for the full company of 150 men. But on the last day, the English opened up heavily on us. We suffered severely and came back with 80 men.

Last night we moved back and settled down to get a good night's sleep. At the front we had next to none. It was noon before the first of us crawled out of our quarters. Half an hour later every man had his mess-tin and was gathered at the cook-house.

At the head of the line of course were the hungriest. There was little Albert Kropp. He is the clearest thinker among us and therefore only a lance-corporal. Next came Müller. He still carries his textbooks with him and dreams of examinations. Then there is Leer, who wears a beard and thinks he's a ladies' man. And then myself, Paul Baümer. All four of us are 19 years old. All four joined up from the same class as volunteers for the war.

Close behind us were our friends. Tjaden, a skinny locksmith who is our age, is the biggest eater of the company. Haie Westhus, also the same age, is a peat-digger. He can easily hold a small loaf of bread in one hand and cover it all. Then there is Detering, a peasant who thinks only of his farm and his wife. Finally comes

Stanislaus Katczinsky, the leader of our group. He is 40 years of age, shrewd, wise, and hard-bitten. He has a remarkable nose for bad weather, good food, and soft jobs.

Kat called to the cook. "Say, Heinrich, open up the soup kitchen. The beans are done."

"Everyone must be there first," the cook said.

Tjaden grinned. "We are all here."

"That may do for you," he said. "But where are the others?"

"They're either in the dressing-station[1] or pushing up daisies."

The cook was quite upset as the facts dawned on him. "And I have cooked for 150 men—"

"Then for once we'll have enough," Kropp said.

"Man, you've got bread and sausage for 150 men?" Tjaden asked. "And tobacco, too?"

"Yes, everything," the cook said.

"Then, each man gets—yes—almost enough for two!" Tjaden said.

"I don't care about the stew," the cook said. "But I can only issue rations for 80 men."

Katczinsky got angry. "You haven't drawn food for 80 men. You've drawn it for the Second Company. We are the Second Company."

There certainly would have been a fight if the company commander hadn't come by. He learned of the dispute and remarked, "Yes, we did have heavy losses yesterday." He looked into the pot. "The beans look good." He looked at us. He knew what we were thinking. He had been one of us, and was promoted from the ranks.

He sniffed the pot again. Then he said, "Bring me a

---

1. **dressing-station**   first-aid station

plate full. Serve all the rations. We can do with them."

Today is a wonderful day. The mail has come, and almost every man has a few letters and papers. We stroll over to the meadow behind the billets.[2]

"Anyone seen Kemmerich lately?" Kropp asks.

"He's up at St. Joseph's," I tell him.

Müller explains that he has a flesh wound in his thigh. It's serious.

We decide to go and see him this afternoon.

Kropp pulls out a letter. "Kantorek sends you his best wishes," he says.

We laugh. Müller throws away his cigarette. "I wish he was here."

Kantorek had been our teacher. He is a stern little man in a gray coat, with a face like a shrew mouse. During our lessons, he would give us long lectures about patriotism. Finally, our whole class volunteered to fight. I can see Kantorek now, as he used to glare at us through his spectacles. "Won't you join up, comrades?" he'd say in a moving voice.

Only one of us hesitated. That was Joseph Behm, a homely fellow. But he let himself be persuaded. Strange to say, Behm was one of the first to fall. He got hit in the eye during an attack, and we left him for dead. In the afternoon, suddenly we heard him call. We saw him crawling about in No Man's Land. He had only been knocked out. Because he couldn't see and was mad with pain, he failed to keep under cover. He was shot down before anyone could get to him.

Naturally, we couldn't blame Kantorek for this. There were thousands of Kantoreks. All of them were convinced that they were acting for the best—in a way

---

2. billets lodgings for members of the armed forces

that cost them nothing.

And that is why they let us down so badly.

For us lads of 18, they ought to have been guides to the world of maturity. They should have led us into the world of work, of duty, of culture, of progress—to the future. We often made fun of them and played jokes on them. But in our hearts we trusted them. They represented authority. And in our minds, that meant a greater insight and a more humane wisdom.

The first death we saw, however, shattered this belief. We had to recognize that our generation was more to be trusted than theirs. They surpassed us only in cleverness. The first bombardment[3] showed us our mistake. Under it, the world as they had taught it to us broke into pieces.

When we arrive at the dressing-station, there is great activity. We ask for Kemmerich. He lies in a large room and receives us with a weak expression of joy. He is also very upset. While he was unconscious someone had stolen his watch.

Müller shakes his head. "I always told you that nobody should carry as good a watch as that."

Müller is not thinking clearly. Otherwise, he would hold his tongue. Anybody can see that Kemmerich will never come out of this place again. Whether he finds his watch or not will make no difference.

"How goes it, Franz?" Kropp asks.

Kemmerich's head sinks. "Not so bad...but I have such a bad pain in my foot."

The bed covering arches over Kemmerich's leg. I kick Müller on the shin. He is about to tell Kemmerich what the orderlies told us outside: Kemmerich has lost

---

3. bombardment a bombing attack

his foot. The leg is amputated. He looks terrible. His face already shows the strained lines that we know so well. They are not so much lines as marks. Under the skin, the life no longer pulses. Death is working through from within.

Müller leans over. "We have brought your things, Franz."

Kemmerich signs with his hands to put them under the bed. Müller does so, and reappears with a pair of airman's boots. They are fine English boots of soft leather that reach up to the knees. Müller is delighted at the sight of them. "Will you be taking them, Franz?"

We three have the same thought. The boots are of no use to him. If they remain here, the orderlies will grab them as soon as he is dead.

"Won't you leave them with us?" Müller goes on.

Kemmerich doesn't want to. They are his most prized possessions.

"Well, we could exchange," Müller suggests.

Still, Kemmerich will not be moved. I step on Müller's foot. He puts the boots back under the bed.

We talk a bit more and then prepare to leave. "Cheerio, Franz."

I promise to come back in the morning. So does Müller. He is thinking of the boots and means to be on the spot.

We go back to the huts. We walk on for a long time. I think of the letter I must write tomorrow to Kemmerich's mother.

"What has Kantorek written to you?" Müller asks Kropp.

Kropp laughs. "We are the Iron Youth."

We all smile bitterly. Yes, that's the way they think, these hundred thousand Kantoreks! Iron Youth! Youth! None of us are more than 20 years old. But young? Youth? That is long ago. We are old folk.

Chapter 2

At home in the drawer of my writing table lies the beginning of a play and a bundle of poems. Many an evening I have worked over them. But that has become so unreal to me that I cannot understand it any more. Our early life is cut off from the moment we came here.

For us young men of 20, everything is very vague. All the older men are linked with their earlier life. They have wives, children, jobs, and interests. They have a background which is so strong that the war cannot wipe it out. We young men, however, have only our parents, and some, perhaps a girl. Besides this, our life did not extend. And of this, nothing remains.

Kantorek would say that we stood on the threshold of life. And so it would seem. We had not taken root yet. The war swept us away. The older men think beyond it. We, however, have been gripped by it and do not know what the end may be. We only know that in some strange and sad way, we have become a waste land.

Once, it was different. When we enlisted, we had no firm plans for the future. We had not yet given thoughts to a career or an occupation. We were still full of vague, romantic ideas about life—and about war. We were trained in the army for ten weeks. In this time, we were more strongly influenced than by ten years at school.

Our class was scattered by threes and fours over different platoons. Kropp, Müller, Kemmerich, and I went to No. 9 platoon under Corporal Himmelstoss. He had the reputation of being the toughest trainer of recruits in the camp. And he was proud of it. He was a small fellow with a foxy, waxed mustache. He had seen 12 years of service and was a postman in civilian life. He had a special dislike of Kropp, Tjaden, Westhus, and me.

I once remade his bed 14 times in one morning. Each time, he had some fault to find and pulled it to pieces. Under his orders I scrubbed out the Corporals' Mess[1] with a tooth-brush. Kropp and I were given the job of clearing the barrack-square of snow with a broom and dust pan. We would have gone on until we were frozen, but a lieutenant accidentally showed up and sent us off. Then he hauled Himmelstoss over the coals. But the result of this was to make Himmelstoss hate us more.

There were many other abuses. Then one Sunday, Kropp and I were lugging a latrine[2]-bucket on a pole across the barrack yard. Himmelstoss came by, all polished and dressed up to go out. He stood in front of us and asked how we liked the job. In spite of ourselves, we tripped and emptied the bucket over his legs.

"This means clink," he yelled.

But Kropp had had enough. "There'll be an inquiry first," he said. "Then we'll unload."

"Mind you how you speak to a non-commissioned[3] officer!" Himmelstoss yelled. "Have you lost your senses? What will you do, anyway?"

"Show you up, Corporal," Kropp said.

Himmelstoss saw that we meant it. Before he dis-

---

1. **Mess** dining hall
2. **latrine** a toilet
3. **non-commissioned** non-com.; non-commissioned officer. A military officer appointed from among enlisted men rather than gaining rank by graduating from military school.

appeared he growled: "You'll drink this!" But that was the end of his authority. After that he left us in peace. He did indeed always refer to us as swine. However, there was a certain respect in his tone.

We were put through every kind of parade-ground soldiering till we often howled with rage. Many of us became ill through it. One man actually died. We became hard, suspicious, pitiless, and tough—and that was good. For these qualities were just what we lacked. Had we gone into the trenches without this training, most of us would certainly have gone mad. We did not break down, but we adapted ourselves. The most important result was it awakened in us a strong, practical sense of *esprit de corps*.[4] In the field it developed into the finest thing that came out of the war—comradeship.

I sit by Kemmerich's bed. He is sinking rapidly. The doctor passes by his bed without once looking at him.

Franz raises himself on the pillow with his elbows. "They have amputated my leg."

I nod. "You must be glad you've come off with that."

He is silent.

I continue. "It might have been both legs, Franz. Wegeler has lost his right arm. That's much worse. Besides, you'll be going home."

He looks at me. "Do you think so?"

"Of course. Once you've gotten over the operation."

He motions for me to bend down. I stoop over him and he whispers: "I don't think so."

"Don't talk rubbish, Franz. What is an amputated leg, anyway? They patch up far worse things than that."

---

4. **esprit de corps** a spirit of loyalty and devotion that members of a group show for one another

For a while he lies still. Then he says, "You can take my boots with you for Müller."

I nod and wonder what to say to encourage him. His mouth has become larger. His teeth stick out and look as though they were made of chalk. The skeleton is working through. In a couple of hours, it will be over.

He is not the first I have seen this way. But we grew up together. That always makes it a bit different.

It grows dark. Kemmerich's face changes color. The mouth moves slowly. I draw near to him. He whispers, "If you find my watch, send it home—"

I do not reply. It's no use. No one can make him feel any better. I am miserable with my helplessness.

Hospital orderlies go back and forth with bottles and pails. One of them comes up, looks at Kemmerich, and goes away. You can see that he is waiting for the bed.

I bend over Franz and talk to him as though that could save him. "Perhaps you will go to the home at Klosterberg. Then you can look from the windows to the trees on the horizon. It is the loveliest time of year."

I lean down over Franz's face which lies in the shadow. He still breathes, lightly. His face is wet. He is crying. What a fine mess I have made of it with my foolish talk!

An hour passes. He is entirely alone now with his little life of 19 years, and cries because it leaves him. This is the most disturbing parting that I have ever seen.

Suddenly, Kemmerich groans and begins to gurgle. I stumble outside and demand, "Where is the doctor?"

As I catch sight of the white apron, I grab hold of it.

"Come quick; Franz Kemmerich is dying."

The doctor frees himself and tells a hospital-orderly, "You see to it." He hurries off to the operating room.

We are by Kemmerich's bed. He is dead. The face is still wet from the tears. The orderly pokes me. "We must take him away. Outside, they are lying on the floor."

I collect Kemmerich's things and leave. Outside the door, I am grateful for the darkness and the wind. Thoughts of girls, of flowery meadows, of white clouds come into my head. My feet move forward. I run.

Müller stands in front of the hut waiting for me. I give him the boots. We go in and he tries them on. They fit well. He looks among his supplies and offers me a fine piece of sausage. With it goes hot tea and rum.

Chapter 3

Reinforcements have arrived. Some of them are old hands. But there are 25 men of a later draft from the base. They are about two years younger than us. Kropp nudges me. "Seen the infants?" he says.

I nod. We look over the recruits and feel as if we're stone-age veterans.

Katczinsky joins us. We go over to the new men, who are already being given gas masks and coffee.

"A long time since you've had anything decent to eat?" Kat asks one of the youngsters.

He frowns. "For breakfast, turnip-bread; lunch, turnip-stew; dinner, turnip-cutlets and turnip salad."

Kat gives a knowing whistle. "What do you say to haricot beans? Have some?"

The youngster turns red. "You can't kid me."

Katczinsky just says, "Fetch your mess-tin."

We follow along. He takes us to a tub beside his straw sack. Sure enough, it is half full of beef and beans.

We are surprised. "Great guts, Kat, how did you come by that?" I ask him.

"The cook was glad I took it," he answers. "I gave him three pieces of parachute-silk for it."

He gives the youngster a portion. "Next time you come with your mess-tin, have a cigar or some tobacco in your other hand. Get me?" Kat says. Then he turns to us. "You get off scot free, of course."

We couldn't do without Katczinsky. He has a sixth sense. There are such people everywhere. Every company has one or two. Katczinsky is the smartest I know.

For example, we land at night at some unknown

spot. It's a sorry hole that has been eaten out to the very walls. The beds are just a couple of wooden beams with wire netting stretched over them.

Wire netting is hard. And there's nothing to put over it. Our waterproof sheets are too thin. We use our blankets to cover ourselves.

Kat looks at the place. Then he says to Haie Westhus, "Come with me." They go off to explore. Half an hour later, they are back again with arms full of straw. Kat has found a horse-box with straw in it. Now we might sleep if we weren't so hungry.

Kropp talks to another soldier who has been some time in this neighborhood.

The man says, "There's nothing to be had here. You won't find so much as a crust of bread here."

"Aren't there any people living around here?" Kropp asks.

"Yes, a few," the man says. "But they hang around the cook-house and beg."

Kat has put on his cap. "Where to, Kat?" I ask.

"Just to explore the place a bit." He strolls off. The soldier grins with scorn. "Go ahead and explore. But don't hurt yourself carrying what you find."

We are just dozing off when the door opens and Kat appears. I think I must be dreaming. He has two loaves of bread under his arm. In his hand he has a bloodstained sandbag full of horse-flesh.

The soldier's pipe drops from his mouth. He feels the bread. "Real bread, by God, and still hot."

Kat doesn't explain. He has the bread. The rest doesn't matter. "Cut some wood," he says to Haie. Then he brings out a frying pan from under his coat. He takes a handful of salt and some fat from his pocket. He has thought of everything. Haie makes a fire on the floor. We climb out of bed.

The soldier hesitates. He wonders if he should praise Kat and gain a little for himself. But Kat doesn't even see him. He might as well be thin air. The soldier goes off angrily.

We have settled ourselves on the sunny side of the hut. Kat sits beside me. He likes to talk. Today we have done an hour's saluting drill because Tjaden failed to salute a major smartly enough. Kat can't get it out of his head.

"You take it from me," he says. "We are losing the war because we can salute too well."

Kropp comes up, and the two begin to argue. At the same time, they make a bet on the result of an air fight that's going on above us. Kat won't budge from his opinion, which he sets to rhyme:

Give 'em all the same grub and all the same pay
And the war would be over and done in a day.

Kropp, on the other hand, is a thinker. He says that a declaration of war should be a kind of popular festival. There should be tickets sold, and bands, like a bull fight. Then put the ministers and generals of the two countries in the arena. Arm them with clubs, and they can have it out. Whoever survives, his country wins. That would be much simpler and fairer than this arrangement where the wrong people do the fighting.

The subject is dropped. The conversation turns to other things. Meanwhile, the German airplane has been shot down. Like a comet, it bursts into a streamer of smoke and falls from the sky. Kropp has lost the bet. He counts out the money from his wallet.

Here, Tjaden comes up with a flushed face. He is so excited that he stutters. "Himmelstoss is on his way," he stammers. "He's coming to the front!"

Tjaden has a special grudge against Himmelstoss. He treated Tjaden even worse than the rest of us. Meanwhile, Haie sits down beside us. He winks at me and rubs his paws thoughtfully. We once spent the finest day of our army life together—the day before we left for the front. We were to leave the next morning early. In the evening, we prepared to square accounts with Himmelstoss.

We had sworn for weeks to do this. We decided to give him a good hiding. He went out one evening as he often did. To return to the barracks, he had to go along a dark, empty road. There we waited for him behind a pile of stones. I had a bed cover with me.

When he arrived, we made a quick leap and threw the bed cover over his head and arms. Haie Westhus hit him first—hard. Himmelstoss fell down and rolled five yards. He began to yell.

We pressed his head hard onto a pillow we had brought. Tjaden unbuttoned Himmelstoss's pants and pulled them down. Then we took turns smacking him with a whip we'd brought. Finally, Haie stood him up again. He gave him one last shot upon the ear.

Himmelstoss toppled over. Then he yelled and made off on all fours. His striped postman's backside gleamed in the moonlight.

We disappeared at full speed. He never discovered who he had to thank for the business.

Chapter 4

We have to go up on wiring detail.[1] The trucks roll up after dark. We climb in. It is a warm evening. We stand jammed in together, shoulder to shoulder. There is no room to sit. But we do not expect that. Müller is in a good mood for once. He is wearing his new boots.

The trucks arrive at the artillery[2] lines. The guns are hidden by bushes so that enemy planes cannot spot them. The air becomes thick with the smoke of the guns and the fog. The fumes of powder taste bitter on the tongue. The roar of the guns makes our truck stagger. We are not in the front line, but in every face it can be read: This is the front. Now we are within its embrace.

It is not fear. We have become thick-skinned. Only the young recruits are upset.

Three guns open fire close beside us. The burst of flame shoots across the fog. The guns roar and boom. We shiver. We are glad to think that we shall be back in the huts early in the morning.

We pass by soup kitchens and arrive in the woods. We climb out. The trucks are to collect us in the morning before dawn. Mist and smoke lie chest-high over the fields. The moon is shining. Along the road, troops file. Their helmets gleam softly in the moonlight. The heads and rifles stand out above the white mist.

Guns and munition[3] wagons are moving along a

---

1. **wiring detail**   putting up barbed-wire fences to keep the enemy from moving forward
2. **artillery**   large weapons
3. **munition**   ammunition

cross-road. The backs of the horses shine in the moon-light. Their movements are beautiful. They toss their heads and their eyes gleam. The riders in their steel helmets resemble knights. It is strangely beautiful.

We push on to the supply dump.[4] Some of us load our shoulders with pointed and twisted iron stakes. Others thrust smooth iron rods through rolls of wire.

The ground becomes more broken. From ahead come the warnings: "Look out: deep shell-hole on the left." "Mind: trenches."

There are some shell-smashed trucks on the road. It has become pitch dark. We move around a small wood and then have the front-line right before us.

A red glow spreads across the sky from one end to the other. French rockets go up. They unfold a silk parachute to the air and drift slowly down. They light up everything as bright as day. Their light shines on us, and we see our shadows sharply outlined on the ground.

"Bombardment," says Kat.

The thunder of the guns swells to a single heavy roar. Then it breaks up again into separate explosions. The dry bursts of the machine-guns rattle.

At regular periods, we ram in the iron stakes. Two men hold a roll and the others spool off the barbed wire. I am not used to unrolling it and tear my hand.

After a few hours it is done. But there is still some time before the trucks come. Most of us lie down and sleep. I try, but it has turned too chilly.

A shell lands behind us. Some recruits jump up, ter-rified. A few minutes later, another comes over, nearer this time. Kat knocks out his pipe. "We're in for it."

Then it begins for real. We crawl away as well as we

---

4. **dump** storehouse

can. The next one lands quite close. Two fellows cry out. Green rockets shoot up on the sky-line. Barrage. The mud flies high; shell fragments whiz past. The crack of the guns is heard long after the roar of the explosions.

Beside us lies a fair-headed recruit in complete terror. He has buried his face in his hands; his helmet has fallen off. I grab it and try to put it back on his head. He looks up and pushes the helmet off. Like a child, he creeps under my arm, his head close to my chest. The little shoulders heave. Shoulders like Kemmerich's. I let him be.

It's got someone pretty badly. Cries are heard between the explosions.

At last it grows quiet. I sit up and shake the recruit by the shoulder. "All over, kid! It's all right this time."

He looks around him in a daze. "You'll get used to it soon," I tell him.

He moves off. Things become quieter, but the cries do not stop. It is not men. They could not cry so terribly.

"Wounded horses," Kat says.

It is impossible to take. It is the moaning of the world. We are pale. Detering stands up. "God! For God's sake! Shoot them."

He is a farmer and very fond of horses. It gets under his skin. The screaming of the beasts becomes louder. Detering raves and yells out, "Shoot them, can't you?"

"They must look after the men first," says Kat quietly.

We can bear almost anything. But now the sweat breaks out on us. We must get up and run where these cries can no longer be heard. And it is only horses.

Then single shots crack out. One horse drops—then another. But it is still not the end. The men cannot stop the wounded beasts from flying about in their pain. The last one props itself on its front legs and drags itself around in a circle like a merry-go-round. It appears to have a broken back. A soldier runs up and shoots it. Slowly, it sinks to the ground.

We take our hands from our ears. The cries are silenced. Only a long-drawn, dying sigh still hangs in the air. Detering walks up and down cursing. "I tell you, it is terrible to use horses in war."

We go back. It is time we returned to the trucks. The sky has become brighter. It's three o'clock in the morning. The breeze is fresh and cool. We trudge in single file through the trenches and shell-holes and come again to the zone of mist. The little wood reappears. We know every foot of ground here. There's the cemetery with the mounds and the black crosses.

That moment, it breaks out behind us, swells, roars, and thunders. We duck down. A cloud of flame shoots up 100 yards ahead of us.

The next minute, there is a second explosion. Part of the wood rises slowly in the air. Three or four trees sail up and then crash to pieces.

"Take cover!" somebody yells.

The only cover is the graveyard and the mounds. We stumble in the dark. Every man lies behind a mound.

The flames of the explosions light up the graveyard. There is no escape anywhere. The wood vanishes. It is torn to pieces. We must stay here in the graveyard.

The earth bursts before us. I feel a smack. My sleeve is torn away by a splinter. I shut my fist. No pain. I feel the arm all over. It is grazed but sound. Now a crack on the skull. I begin to black out. Quickly, the thought comes to me: Don't faint! I sink down into the black broth and immediately come up again.

I wipe the mud out of my eyes. A hole is torn up in front of me. Shells hardly ever land in the same hole twice. I'll get into it. With one lunge, I shoot as flat as a fish over the ground. I feel something on the left. I shove in beside it; it gives way. I draw it over me for cover.

I open my eyes. My fingers grasp a sleeve, an arm. A wounded man? I yell to him—no answer. A dead man. My hand gropes farther, and I feel splinters of wood. Now I remember again that we are lying in the graveyard. I just crawl still farther under the coffin. It shall protect me though Death himself lies in it.

Before me gapes the shell-hole. With one leap I must be in it. There, I get a smack in the face. A hand clamps on my shoulder and shakes me. I turn my head and stare in the face of Katczinsky. He has his mouth open and is yelling. I hear nothing. He rattles me and comes nearer. His voice reaches me: "Gas—Gas—Pass it on."

I grab for my gas mask. Some distance from me there lies someone. I call, I lean toward him—he doesn't see. It's a recruit. I look at Kat desperately; he has his mask on. I pull out mine, too. My helmet falls to one side. I slip the mask over my face. I reach the man. His satchel is near me. I grab his mask and pull it over his head. He understands. I let go and drop into the shell-hole.

Someone plumps down behind me, then another. It is Kat, Kropp, and someone else. All four of us lie there in suspense and breathe as lightly as possible.

These first minutes with the mask decide between life and death. Is it air-tight? Cautiously, with my mouth on the valve, I breathe. The gas still creeps over the ground and sinks into all hollows. I nudge Kat. It

is better to crawl out and lie on top than to stay where the gas collects most. But we don't get as far as that. A second bombardment begins.

With a crash, something black bears down on us. It lands close beside us. It is a coffin.

I see Kat and I crawl across. The coffin has hit the fourth man in our hole on his outstretched arm. He tries to tear off his gas mask. Kropp seizes him just in time. Kat and I free the wounded arm. We tear the coffin lid off and toss the corpse out. Then we try to loosen the under part. Finally, the coffin gives way.

Kat takes a piece of the lid and places it under the shattered arm. We wrap all our bandages around it. For the moment, we can do no more.

Inside the gas mask, my head booms. My lungs are tight. They breathe the same hot, used-up air. The veins on my temples are swollen. I feel I am suffocating.

I climb over the edge of the shell-hole. Something stands up a few yards ahead. I clear the goggles and peer through them. The man there no longer wears his mask.

I wait a few seconds. He has not collapsed. He looks around and walks a few paces. I tear my mask off and fall down. The air streams into me like cold water.

The shelling has stopped. I turn towards the others and beckon them. They take off their masks. We lift up the wounded man, one taking his splintered arm. And so, we stumble off quickly.

The graveyard is a mass of wreckage. Coffins and corpses lie everywhere. They have been killed again. But each one that was flung up saved one of us.

Someone lies in front of us. We stop, but Kropp goes on with the wounded man. The man on the ground is a recruit. His hip is covered with blood.

"Where did it get you, comrade?" Kat asks.

His eyes move. He is too weak to answer. We slit open his pants carefully. He groans. "Gently, gently."

We lay the hip bare. It is one mass of mincemeat and bone splinters. The joint has been hit. This lad won't walk any more.

Kat spreads out two wads of dressing as wide as possible so that they will cover the wound. Then he takes a bandage from a dead man's pocket, and we carefully bind the wound. I say to the youngster, "We're going for a stretcher now—"

Then he opens his mouth and whispers, "Stay here—"

"We'll be back again soon," Kat says. "We are only going to get a stretcher for you."

We don't know if he understands. He whimpers like a child. "Don't go away—"

Kat looks around. "Shouldn't we just take a revolver and put an end to it?" he whispers.

The youngster will barely survive the carrying. At the most, he will only last a few days. What he has gone through so far is nothing compared to what he's in for until he dies. Now he feels nothing. In an hour he will become one screaming bundle of horrible pain. Every day that he can live will be a howling torture.

I nod. "Yes, we ought to put him out of his misery."

He stands still a moment. He has made up his mind. We look round—but we are no longer alone. A little group is gathering. We get a stretcher.

Kat shakes his head. "Such a kid—" He repeats it. "Young innocents."

Our losses are less than we expected—five killed and eight wounded. It was in fact quite a short bombardment. Two of our dead lie in the upturned graves. We merely throw the earth in on them.

We go back. The wounded are taken to the dressing-station. It begins to rain. An hour later, we reach our trucks and climb in. There is more room now.

The rain becomes heavier. We take out waterproof sheets and spread them over our heads. The trucks bump in the holes, and we rock in a half-sleep.

The rain falls on our heads and on the heads of the dead up in the line. It falls on the body of the little recruit with the hip wound. It falls on Kemmerich's grave. And it falls in our hearts.

Chapter 5

The rumor has come true. Himmelstoss has come. He appeared yesterday. We've already heard the well-known voice. He seems to have overdone it with a couple of young recruits on the field at home. Unknown to him, the son of the local official was watching. That cooked his goose.

He will get some surprises here. Tjaden has been thinking for hours what to say to him. Haie looks thoughtfully at his great paws and winks at me. Kropp and Müller are amusing themselves. From somewhere or other, Kropp has bagged for himself a mess-tin full of beans. Müller squints with hungry eyes into it. But he checks himself. He says, "Albert, what would you do if it were suddenly peace-time again?"

"There won't be any peace-time," says Albert bluntly.

"Well, but if—what would you do?"

"Clear out of this!" growls Kropp.

"Of course. And then what?"

"Get drunk," says Albert.

"Don't talk rot, I mean seriously—"

"So do I," Kropp says. "What else should a man do?"

Kat becomes interested. "You might get drunk first, of course," he says. "But then you'd take the next train for home and mother. Peace-time, man, Albert—"

He fumbles in his oil-cloth pocketbook for a photograph. He shows it all round. "My old woman!" Then he puts it back and swears. "Damned lousy war—"

"It's all very well for you to talk," I tell him. "You have a wife and children."

"True," he nods. "And I have to see to it that they have something to eat."

We laugh. "They won't lack for that, Kat. You'd get it from somewhere."

Müller gives himself no peace. He wakes Haie Westhus out of his dream. "Haie, what would you do if it was peace-time?"

Haie shakes his freckled head. "You mean when the war is over?"

"Exactly. You've said it."

A pause. Then Haie says, "If I were a non-com, I'd stay with the Prussians and serve out my time."

"Haie, you've got a screw loose, surely!" I say.

"Have you ever dug peat?" he says good-naturedly. "You try it."

"It can't be worse than digging trenches," I say.

Haie grins. "It lasts longer though. And there's no getting out of it either."

He goes on. "In the army in peace-time you have nothing to trouble about. Your food is found every day, or else you complain. You have a bed, every week clean underwear like a perfect gent. You do your non-com's duty, you have a good suit of clothes. In the evening, you're a free man and go off to the pub."

"You'll never be a non-com though, Haie," Kat says.

Haie looks at him sadly and is silent. His thoughts linger over clear evenings in autumn.

"What would you do, Tjaden?" asks Kropp.

Tjaden thinks of one thing only. "See to it that Himmelstoss didn't get past me."

"And you, Detering!" Müller asks.

Detering is sparing with his words. But on this subject he speaks. He looks at the sky and says only one sentence. "I would go straight on with the harvesting." Then he gets up and walks off.

At this moment, Himmelstoss appears. He comes straight up to our group. Tjaden's face turns red, and he shuts his eyes in excitement. Himmelstoss is a little hesitant. His walk becomes slower. Then he marches up to us. No one makes any motion to stand up. Kropp looks up at him with interest.

He continues to stand in front of us and wait. No one says anything. He launches a "Well!"

A couple of seconds go by. Himmelstoss doesn't quite know what to do. "Well, you here too?" he finally says to Kropp.

"A bit longer than you, I think," Kropp replies.

"You don't recognize me any more, what?"

Tjaden now opens his eyes. "I do, though."

Himmelstoss turns to him. "Tjaden, isn't it?"

Tjaden lifts his head. "And do you know what you are?"

Himmelstoss is upset. "Since when have we become so familiar? I don't remember that we ever slept in the gutter together."

He has no idea what to make of the situation. He didn't expect this open hostility. The question about the gutter makes Tjaden so mad that he becomes almost witty. "No, you slept there by yourself," he says.

Himmelstoss begins to boil. But Tjaden gets in ahead of him. "Wouldn't you like to know what you are? I've been wanting to tell you that for a long time." He spits out, "Dirty hound!"

Himmelstoss lets fly too, now. "What's that, you muck-rake, you dirty peat-stealer? Stand up. Bring your heels together when your superior officer speaks to you."

Tjaden waves him off. "You take a run and jump at yourself, Himmelstoss."

"Tjaden, I command you, as your superior officer. Stand up!"

"Anything else you would like?" Tjaden asks.

"Will you obey my order or not?"

Tjaden replies in a very familiar way. Air comes out of his backside.

"I'll have you court-martialed,"[1] Himmelstoss storms.

We watch him disappear in the direction of the Orderly Room.[2] Haie and Tjaden burst into laughter.

Kat is troubled. "If he reports you, it will be pretty serious."

"Do you think he will?" Tjaden asks.

"Sure to," I say.

"The least you'll get will be five days close arrest," Kat says.

That doesn't worry Tjaden. "Five days clink are five days rest. For the time being, the war will be over so far as I am concerned."

Tjaden is a cheerful soul. There aren't any worries for him. He goes off with Haie and Leer so that they won't find him.

Müller hasn't finished yet. He tackles Kropp again.

"Albert, if you were really at home now, what would you do?"

Kropp is happy now and ready to answer. "How many of us were there in the class exactly?"

We count up. Out of 20, 7 are dead, 4 wounded, 1 in a mad-house. That makes 12.

"What will happen to us when we go back?" Müller wonders.

Kropp gives a shrug. "I don't know. Let's get back first. Then we'll find out."

We are all at a loss. "What could we do?" I ask.

---

1. **court-martialed** charged with breaking military law
2. **Orderly Room** unit headquarters

"I don't want to do anything," Kropp replies wearily. "You'll be dead one day, so what does it matter? I don't think we'll ever go back."

"When I hear the word 'peace-time,' it goes to my head. If it really came, I think I would do something worth lying in the muck for. But I can't imagine anything."

All at once, everything seems to be confused and hopeless.

"The war has ruined us for everything," Albert says.

He is right. We were 18 and had begun to love life, and we had to shoot it to pieces. We are cut off from life. We believe in such things no longer. We believe in the war.

Himmelstoss returns, accompanied by a fat sergeant-major. We get up.

"Where's Tjaden?" the sergeant puffs.

No one knows, of course. "You know very well," Himmelstoss says angrily. "You won't say, that's the fact of the matter. Out with it!"

Fatty looks around, but Tjaden is not to be seen. "Tjaden will report at the Orderly Room in ten minutes."

Then he steams off with Himmelstoss behind him.

I go into the hut and put Tjaden wise. He disappears.

Half an hour later, Himmelstoss is back again. He asks for Tjaden. We shrug our shoulders.

Kropp lies back on the grass and speaks. "Have you ever been out here before?"

"It's none of your business," Himmelstoss says.

"See up there where those little white clouds are," Kropp says. "Those are anti-aircraft. We were over there yesterday. Five dead and eight wounded. And that's nothing. Next time you'll go with us. And before they die, the fellows will come up to you and click their heels. 'Please may I go? May I hop it?' they'll say. 'We've been waiting here a long time for someone like you.'"

Himmelstoss disappears like a comet.

"Next time, I'll let fly," I say to Albert.

But that is the end. The case comes up for trial in the evening. In the Orderly Room sits our lieutenant, Bertink. He calls us in one after another.

I have to appear as a witness and explain the reason for Tjaden's behavior toward Himmelstoss. His treatment of Tjaden back in training is brought up. Tjaden testifies, too. The ruling is that he will serve three days' open arrest. Kropp gets one day.

Open arrest is quite pleasant. The clink was once a fowl-house. There we can visit the prisoners. Close arrest would have meant the cellar.

They used to tie us to a tree, but that is not allowed now. In many ways, we are treated like men.

An hour later, Tjaden and Kropp are settled in behind their wire-netting. We make our way to them. Then we play cards far into the night. Tjaden wins of course, the lucky stiff.

When we break it up, Kat says to me, "What do you say to some roast goose?"

"Not bad," I agree.

We climb up on a munition-wagon. The ride costs us two cigarettes. Kat has marked the spot exactly. The shed belongs to a regimental headquarters. I agree to get the goose and receive my instructions.

Kat lifts me up. I rest my foot in his hands and climb over the wall. Kat keeps watch below.

The goose puts up a fight. But at last I grab it and

toss it over the wall. Quickly, I let myself drop. Kat and I run off. In a while, we reach the deserted shack that we use for such purposes. We make a fire.

Kat plucks and cleans the goose. We put the feathers carefully to one side. We intend to make cushions out of them. The sound of the gun-fire from the front reaches into our shack.

We sit opposite one another, Kat and I. Two soldiers in shabby coats, cooking a goose in the middle of the night. We don't talk much. But I believe we have a more complete understanding than even lovers have.

Finally, after a long time, Kat says, "It's done."

We take out our forks and pocket-knives, and each cuts off a leg. With it, we have army bread dipped in gravy. We eat slowly and with pleasure. We are brothers, and offer one another the choicest pieces. Afterwards, there is still a lot left.

"How would it be, Kat, if we took a bit to Kropp and Tjaden?"

"Sure," says he.

We go off to the clink to waken them. Kropp and Tjaden take us for magicians. Then they get busy with their teeth.

"May I never forget you!" Tjaden says.

We go to our hut. Again there is the lofty sky with the stars and the oncoming dawn. I pass beneath it, a soldier with big boots and a full belly. By my side goes Kat, my comrade.

The outlines of the huts are upon us in the dawn like a dark, deep sleep.

Chapter 6

There are rumors of an offensive.[1] We go up to the front two days earlier than usual. On the way, we pass a shelled schoolhouse. Stacked up against one side of it is a high double wall of brand-new coffins. They still smell of pine and the forest. There are at least 100.

"That's a good preparation for the offensive," says Müller, shocked.

"They're for us," growls Detering.

"Don't talk rot," Kat says to him angrily.

"You be thankful if you get so much as a coffin," Tjaden grins. "They'll slip you a waterproof sheet for your old corpse."

The others make jokes too—nasty jokes—but what else can a man do? The coffins are really for us. The organization is excellent in that kind of thing.

We are now in low spirits. We have been in the dugouts for two hours. Now our own shells begin to fall in the trench. This is the third time in four weeks. If it were simply a mistake in aim, no one would say anything. But the truth is that the barrels are worn out. The shots are often so uncertain that they land within our lines. Tonight, two of our men were wounded by our own guns.

We must look out for our bread. We have seen many more rats lately because the trenches are no longer in good condition. Detering says it is a sure sign of a coming bombardment.

The rats here are quite disgusting. They are so

---

1. **offensive** an attack

fat—the kind we call corpse-rats. They have shocking, evil, naked faces. It makes one sick to see their long, nude tails.

They seem to be very hungry. Almost every man has had his bread chewed. Kropp wrapped his in his waterproof sheet and put it under his head. But he cannot sleep because they run over his face to get at it.

At last we put a stop to it. We cannot afford to throw the bread away. Then we would have nothing left to eat in the morning. So we carefully cut off the bits of bread that the animals have chewed.

The slices we cut off are piled together in the middle of the floor. Each man takes out his spade and lies down prepared to strike. Detering, Kropp, and Kat hold their flashlights ready.

After a few minutes, we hear the sound of many little feet. Then the torches switch on and every man strikes at the heap. The rats scatter with a rush. The results are good. We toss the bits of rat over the parapet[2] and again lie in wait.

Several times we repeat the steps. At last the beasts get wise to it. Or perhaps they have smelled the blood. They return no more. Still, before morning the rest of the bread on the floor has been carried off.

We have tired faces and avoid each other's eyes. "It will be like the Battle of the Somme," says Kat gloomily. "There we were shelled steadily for seven days and nights." Kat has lost all his fun since we have been here. That is bad, for Kat is an old front-hog and can smell what is coming.

Day after day passes. At night, I squat in the listening-post. Above me, the rockets shoot up and float down again. I am tense; my heart thumps.

---

2. parapet   a wall of earth built to protect a trench

Nothing happens. I am relieved. Gradually, we grow calmer and play cards continually. Perhaps we will be lucky.

We wake up in the middle of the night. The earth booms. Heavy fire is falling on us. We crouch into corners. Each man lays hold of his things and looks again every minute to reassure himself that they are still there. The dug-out heaves. The night roars and flashes.

Slowly, the gray light trickles into the post and pales the flashes of the shells. Morning is come. The exploding mines mix with the gunfire.

The reliefs go out. The observers stagger in, covered with dirt and trembling. One lies down in silence in the corner and eats. The other, an older man of the new draft, sobs. Twice he has been flung over the parapet by the blast of the explosions. Still, he has only suffered shell-shock.

The recruits are eyeing him. We must watch them. These things are catching, already some lips begin to quiver. It is good that it is growing daylight. Perhaps the attack will come before noon.

The attack does not come. But the bombardment continues. We are gradually made numb. Hardly a man speaks. We cannot make ourselves heard.

Our company commander scrambles in. He reports that two dug-outs are gone. The recruits calm themselves when they see him. He says that an attempt will be made to bring up food this evening.

That sounds reassuring. Now the outside world seems to draw a little nearer. If food can be brought up, the recruits think, then it can't really be so bad.

However, no one gets through. Not even a fly is small enough to get through such a barrage.[3]

---

3. barrage prolonged bombing

We pull in our belts tighter and chew every mouthful three times as long. Still, the food does not last out. We are very hungry. I take out a scrap of bread, eat the white, and put the crust back in my knapsack. From time to time, I nibble at it.

Night again. We are deadened by the strain. Suddenly, the nearer explosions stop. The shelling continues, but it falls behind us. Our trench is free. We grab the hand-grenades, pitch them out in front of the dug-out, and jump after them. The bombardment has stopped and a heavy barrage now falls behind us. The attack has come.

No one would believe that in this howling waste there could still be men. But steel helmets now appear on all sides out of the trench. Fifty yards from us, a machine-gun is already in position and barking.

We see the storm-troops coming. Our artillery opens fire. Machine-guns rattle; rifles crack. The charge works its way across. Haie and Kropp begin with the hand-grenades. They throw them as fast as they can. Haie throws 75 yards, Kropp 60. The distance is important. They enemy cannot do much before they are within 40 yards.

We recognize the smooth, distorted faces, the helmets. They are French. They have already suffered heavily when they reach the remainder of the barbed-wire barriers. A whole line has gone down before our machine-guns. Then we have a let up and they come nearer.

The moment we are about to retreat, three faces rise up from the ground in front of us. Under one of the helmets is a dark pointed beard and two eyes that are fixed on me. I raise my hand. But I cannot throw the grenade into those strange eyes. For one moment, the whole slaughter whirls like a circus around me. And these two eyes alone are still. Then the head rises up, a hand, a movement. My hand-grenade flies through the air and into him.

We have become wild beasts. We do not fight. We defend ourselves against death. It is not against men that we fling our bombs. What do we know of men in this moment when Death is hunting us down? Now for the first time in three days, we can see his face. We feel a mad anger. No longer do we lie helpless. We can destroy and kill to save ourselves—and to be revenged.

Crouching like cats, we run on. We are overwhelmed by this wave that bears us along. It turns us into thugs, into murderers, into devils. If your own father came over with them you would not hesitate to fling a bomb at him.

The forward trenches have been abandoned. Are they still trenches? They are blown to pieces. They are only broken bits of trenches, holes linked by cracks. But the enemies' losses increase. They did not count on so much resistance.

It is nearly noon. The sun blazes hotly. The sweat stings in our eyes. We wipe it off on our sleeves, and there is often blood with it. At last, we reach a trench that is in somewhat better condition. It is manned and ready for the counter-attack. It receives us. Our guns open in full blast and cut off the enemy attack.

The lines behind us stop. They can advance no farther. The attack is crushed by our artillery. We watch. The fire lifts a hundred yards, and we break forward. Beside me, a lance-corporal has his head torn off. He runs a few steps more while the blood spouts from his neck like a fountain.

It does not quite come to hand-to-hand fighting.

They are driven back. We arrive once again at our shattered trench and pass beyond it.

Oh, this turning back again! We reach shelter and yearn to creep in and disappear. But instead we must turn round and plunge again into the horror. We are swept forward again, powerless, madly savage and raging. We will kill, for they are still our mortal enemies. Their rifles and bombs are aimed against us. If we don't destroy them, they will destroy us.

Suddenly, we reach the enemy line. We reach it almost at the same time as they. In this way, we suffer few losses. A machine-gun barks, but is silenced with a bomb. Still, the few seconds have been enough to give us five stomach wounds. Kat smashes the face of one of the machine-gunners. We bayonet the others before they have time to get out their bombs. Then we thirstily drink the water they have for cooling the gun.

The fight stops. We lose touch with the enemy. We cannot stay here long. We must retire under cover of our artillery to our own position. We dive into the nearest dugouts to grab tins of corned beef and butter. Then we clear out.

We get back pretty well. There is no further attack by the enemy. We lie for an hour panting and resting before anyone speaks. We are so played out that we do not think of the food. Then gradually we become something like men again.

The corned beef over there is famous along the whole front. We bagged five tins. The fellows over there are well looked after. They fare much better than us, poor starving wretches. They can get all the meat they want. Haie has scored a thin loaf of white French bread. It is a bit bloody at one corner, but that can be cut off.

It is a good thing that we have something decent to

eat. Food can save our lives. That is why we are so greedy for it.

It is chilly. I am on watch. I am exhausted, so it is hard for me to be alone with my thoughts. They are not really thoughts. They are memories that in my weakness haunt me.

In our town, there stands a line of poplars by a stream. When we were children, the pure smell of the water and the melody of the wind in the poplars held our fancy.

This memory is calm, but calm is impossible now. That is why these memories awaken sorrow. They belong to another world that is gone from us. Today, we would pass through the scenes of our youth like travelers. We are sad like children and experienced like old men. I believe we are lost.

The days go by. The hours follow one another as a matter of course. Attacks alternate with counter-attacks. Slowly, the dead pile up in the field of craters between the trenches. We are able to bring in most of the wounded that do not lie too far off. But many have long to wait, and we listen to them dying.

The days are hot, and the dead lie unburied. We cannot bring them all in. If we did, we should not know what to do with them. The shells will bury them. Many have their bellies swollen up like balloons.

The sky is blue and without clouds. In the evening, it goes steamy and the heat rises from the earth. When the wind blows toward us, it brings the smell of blood, which is heavy and sweet. This smell of death fills us with nausea and retching.

One morning, two butterflies play in front of a trench. They have red spots on their wings. What can they be looking for here? There is not a plant or a flower for miles. They settle on the teeth of a skull. The birds too are just as carefree. They have long since gotten used to the war.

We need reinforcements. But the recruits give us almost more trouble than they are worth. They are helpless. They fall like flies. Modern trench warfare demands knowledge and experience. A man must have a feeling for the shape of the ground, an ear for the sound and character of the shells. He must be able to decide where they will drop and how to shelter from them.

The young recruits of course know none of these things. They are killed because they hardly can tell shrapnel from high-explosive. They flock together like sheep. Even the wounded are shot down like rabbits by the airmen.

It brings a lump to the throat to see how they go over and run and fall. A man would like to take them by the arm and lead them away from here where they have no business to be. For most of them the uniform is far too big. It hangs on their limbs. Their shoulders are too narrow; their bodies are too slight. No uniform was ever made to these childish measurements.

Between five and ten recruits fall to every old hand.

A surprise gas-attack carries off a lot of them. The have not yet learned what to do. We found one dug-out full of them, with blue heads and black lips. Some of them in a shell-hole took off their masks too soon. They did not know that the gas lies longest in the hollows. When they saw others on top without masks they pulled theirs off too and swallowed enough to burn their lungs. Their condition is hopeless.

In one part of the trench, I suddenly run into

Himmelstoss. We dive into the same dug-out. We are all lying one beside the other, waiting for the charge.

We run out again. Although I am very excited, I suddenly think, "Where's Himmelstoss?" Quickly, I jump back into the dug-out. I find him with a small scratch, lying in a corner pretending to be wounded. He is in a panic. He is new to it, too. But it makes me mad that the young recruits should be out there and he here.

"Get out!" I spit.

He does not move. His lips quiver, his mustache twitches.

"Out!" I repeat.

He draws up his legs, crouches back against the wall, and shows his teeth.

I grab him by the arm and try to pull him up. He barks.

This is too much for me. I grab him by the neck and shake him like a sack. His head jerks from side to side.

"You lump, will you get out—sneak out of it, would you? You swine." I push him toward the door and shove him out head first.

Another wave of soldiers has just come up. A lieutenant is with them. He sees us and yells, "Forward, forward, join in, follow." And the word of command does what my banging could not. Himmelstoss hears the order, looks around him, and follows on.

Bombardment, barrage, curtain-fire, mines, gas, tanks, machine-guns, hand-grenades—words, words. But they hold the horror of the world.

Haie Westhus drags off with a great wound in his back. I can only press his hand. "It's all up, Paul," he groans. And he bites his arm because of the pain.

We see men living with their skulls blown open. We see soldiers run with their two feet cut off. They stagger on their splintered stumps into the next shell-hole. We see men without mouths, without jaws, without faces. We find one man who has held the artery of his arm in his teeth for two hours in order not to bleed to death. Night comes, the shells whine. Life is at an end.

We have just been relieved. It was summer when we came up. The trees were still green. Now it is autumn, and the night is gray and wet. The trucks stop, and we climb out. On either side stand people calling out the numbers of the brigades, the battalions.

Now someone is calling out the number of our company. It is the company commander. We go over to him. I recognize Kat and Albert. We stand together, lean against each other and look at one another.

We hear the number of our company called again and again. He will call it a long time. They do not hear him in the hospitals and shell-holes.

"Second Company, this way!" And then more softly, "Nobody else, Second Company?"

He is silent. Then huskily he says, "Is that all?"

It was still summer when we came up. We were 150 strong. Now we freeze. It is autumn, and the leaves rustle. The voices flutter out weakly— One ... 2 ... 3... and stop at 32. Then the voice asks, "Anyone else?"

It waits and then says, softly, "In squads, Second Company, march easy!"

A short line walks off into the morning. Thirty-two men.

Chapter 7

We have to be re-organized. Our company needs more than 100 reinforcements.

In the meantime, when we are off duty, we loaf around. After a couple of days, Himmelstoss comes up to us. He has had the bounce knocked out of him since he has been in the trenches. He wants to get on good terms with us. I am willing because I saw how he brought Haie Westhus in when he was hit in the back. Besides, he's decent enough to treat us in the canteen[1] when we are out of money. Only Tjaden is still reserved and suspicious.

He is won over, too, however. Himmelstoss tells us that he is taking the place of the sergeant-cook who has gone on leave. As a proof, he produces two pounds of sugar for us and a half-pound of butter especially for Tjaden. He even sees to it that we are detailed the next two or three days to the cook-house for potato and turnip peeling. The grub he gives us there is real officers' food.

Thus, for the moment, we have two things a soldier needs to be happy: good food and rest. That's not too much when one comes to think of it. A few years ago we would have hated ourselves. But now we are almost happy. It is all a habit—even the front-line.

Habit explains why we seem to forget things so quickly. Yesterday we were under fire. Today we laugh and go wandering through the countryside. Tomorrow we go up to the trenches again. We forget nothing really. But as long as we have to stay here in the field, the

---

1. **canteen** bar

44

front line days are past. They sink down in us like a stone. They are too awful for us to be able to think about them at once. If we did that, we should have been destroyed long ago.

We turn into animals when we go up to the line. That is the only thing which brings us through safely. We want to live at any price. So we cannot have feelings which, though proper in peacetime, would be out of place here.

Kemmerich is dead, Haie Westhus is dying. Martens has no legs anymore. Meyer is dead. Max is dead. Beyer is dead. There are 120 wounded men lying somewhere or other. It is an awful business. But what has it to do with us now—we live.

If it were possible for us to save them, then it would be seen how much we cared. But our comrades are dead. We cannot help them. They have their rest—and who knows what is waiting for us? We will make ourselves comfortable. We will eat and drink and smoke so hours are not wasted. Life is short.

The terror of the front sinks deep down when we turn our back upon it. But we do not forget. It's all rot that they put in the war-news about the good humor of the troops. We are in a good humor because otherwise we should go to pieces. Even so, we cannot hold out much longer. Our humor becomes more bitter every month.

Some time ago, there was an army theatre performance near here. Colored posters are still sticking to a fence. With wide eyes, Kropp and I stand in front of it. We can hardly believe such things still exist. A girl in a light summer dress! She is a lovely girl. Beside her stands a man in white pants.

"I have some white pants at home," Albert says.

"White pants," say I, "but a girl like that—"

We look at one another. There's not much to boast of here. Two ragged, dirty uniforms. It is hopeless to compete. So we tear the young man off the fence, taking care not to damage the girl.

The houses in which we are billeted lie near the canal. The houses on our side have been abandoned. On the other side, one sometimes sees women.

In the evening, we go swimming. The women stroll on the bank. Leer calls out to them. Tjaden is more crafty. He runs into the house, gets a loaf of bread, and holds it up.

They nod and tell us to come over. But we don't dare do that. It is forbidden. We call to them that we will come when the guards cannot see us. Tonight.

They understand. The brunette does a two-step. The blond girl twitters: "Bread—good."

We each get hold of a whole army loaf and sausages. That makes a decent present.

We stow the things in our boots and swim for it. We find the house at once. The windows are shuttered. Our boots make a great clatter. The house door opens, and a scared woman cries out.

"Ssh, ssh Camarade—bon ami—" we say and show our packages.

The door opens, and light floods us. We unwrap our parcels and give them to the women. Their eyes shine. It is clear they are hungry.

I hold the arm of the brunette tightly and press my lips into the palm of her hand. Her fingers close round my face. Close about me are her bewildering eyes, the soft brown of her skin and her red lips. Her mouth speaks words I do not understand. The words soothe me to a quietness.

I feel the lips of the brunette and press myself against them. My eyes close. I want it all to fall from me, war and terror, and to awaken young and happy. I think of the girl on the poster and for a moment believe that my life depends on winning her. And if I press ever deeper into the arms that embrace me, perhaps a miracle may happen...

I am called to the Orderly Room. The company commander gives me a leave pass and a travel pass. He wishes me a good journey. I look to see how much leave I have got. Seventeen days—14 days leave and 3 days traveling. It's not enough. I ask whether I cannot have five days for traveling. Bertink points to my pass. I see that I am not to return to the front immediately. After my leave, I have to report for a course of training to a camp on the moors.

The others envy me. Kat gives me good advice. He tells me I ought to try to get a base job. "If you're smart, you'll hang onto it."

I would rather not go for another eight days. We were to stay here that much longer, and it is good here.

Naturally, I have to buy the others drinks at the canteen. We are all a little bit drunk. I become gloomy. I will be away for six weeks. That is lucky of course. But what may happen before I get back? Shall I meet all these fellows again? Already Haie and Kemmerich have gone. Who will the next be?

I look at each of them in turn. Albert sits beside me and smokes. He is cheerful. We have always been together. Opposite squats Kat, with his drooping shoulders and calm voice. Müller, with the projecting teeth and the booming laugh. Tjaden with his mousy eyes. And Leer, who has grown a full beard and looks at least 40.

Over us hangs a thick cloud of smoke. Where would a soldier be without tobacco? The canteen is his place of shelter, and beer is far more than a drink. It is a token that a man can move his limbs and stretch in safety. We drink as if it were a ceremony. How it all rises before a man when he is going away the next morning.

The next morning, after I have been de-loused,[2] I go to the railway station. Albert and Kat come with me. At the station we learn that it will be a couple of hours yet before the train leaves. The other two have to return to duty. We take leave of one another.

"Good luck, Kat. Good luck, Albert."

They go off and wave once or twice. Their figures grow smaller. I know their every step and movement. I would recognize them at any distance. Then they disappear. I sit down on my pack and wait. Suddenly, I have a great wish to be gone.

I lie down on many a station platform. I stand before many a soup-kitchen. I squat on many a bench. Then at last the landscape becomes disturbing, mysterious, and familiar. It glides past with its villages, its cornfields, its orchards, and its barns.

The names of the stations begin to take on meaning. My heart trembles. The train moves onward. I stand at the window and hold onto the frame. In the distance, the shape of the mountain ranges begins to appear. I recognize one clearly. Behind it should lie the town.

Finally, the first houses appear. Then a street crossing. Below there are cyclists, trucks, men. It is a gray street and a gray subway. Then the train stops. There is the station with noise and cries and signboards. I

---

2. **de-loused** rid of lice

pick up my pack and tighten the straps. I take my rifle in my hand and stumble down the steps.

On the platform, I look around. I know no one among all the people hurrying back and forth. A Red Cross sister offers me something to drink. I turn away. She smiles at me too foolishly. She is sure of her own importance. "Just look, I am giving a soldier coffee!" She calls me "Comrade." I will have none of it.

Walking down the street, I know every shop: the grocer's, the druggist's, the baker's. Then at last, I stand before the brown door with the worn latch. My hand grows heavy. I open the door and a strange coolness comes out to meet me. My eyes are dim.

The stairs creak under my boots. Upstairs, a door rattles. Someone is looking over the railing. It is the kitchen door that was opened. They are cooking potato-cakes. The house smells of it. And today is Saturday. That will be my sister leaning over. For a moment, I am shy and lower my head. Then I take off my helmet and look up. Yes, it is my eldest sister.

"Paul," she cries. "Paul—"

I nod. My pack bumps on the stairs. My rifle is so heavy.

She pulls a door open and calls, "Mother, Mother, Paul is here."

I lean against the wall. I grip my helmet and rifle. I hold them as tightly as I can. But I cannot take another step. The staircase fades before my eyes. I support myself with the butt of my rifle against my feet. I clench my teeth fiercely, but I cannot speak a word. My sister's call has made me powerless. I can do nothing. I struggle to make myself laugh, to speak. But no word comes. So I stand on the steps miserable and helpless. Against my will, the tears run down my cheeks.

My sister comes back and says, "Why, what is the matter?"

I pull myself together and stagger on to the landing. I lean my rifle in a corner. I set my pack against the wall and place my helmet on it. Then I fling down my equipment and baggage. I say fiercely, "Bring me a handkerchief."

She gives me one, and I dry my face. Now I hear my mother's voice. It comes from the bedroom.

"Is she in bed?" I ask my sister.

"She is ill—" she replies.

I go in to her and say as calmly as I can, "Here I am, Mother."

She lies still in the dim light. Then she asks, "Are you wounded?"

"No, I have got leave."

My mother is very pale. I am afraid to make a light.

"Here I lie now," says she. "And I cry instead of being glad."

"Are you sick, Mother?" I ask.

"I am going to get up a little today," she says. She turns to my sister. "Put out that jar of whortleberries. You like that, don't you?" she asks me.

"Yes, Mother. I haven't had any for a long time."

"Sit here beside me," my mother says.

She looks at me. Her hands are white and thin compared with mine. We say very little, and I am thankful that she asks nothing. What should I say? Everything I could have wished for has happened. I have come out of it safely and sit here beside her. And in the kitchen stands my sister preparing supper and singing.

I sit by her bed and look out the window. The chestnut trees in the beer garden opposite glow in brown and gold. I breathe deeply and say over to myself, "You are at home, you are at home." But a sense of

strangeness will not leave me. I cannot feel at home amongst these things. There is my mother, there is my sister, there is our piano. But I am not myself here. There is a distance, a veil between us.

I go and bring my pack to the bedside and turn out the things I have brought. There is a whole block of cheese that Kat gave me, two loaves of bread, two tins of sausage, and some butter and rice.

"I suppose you can make some use of that—"

They nod.

"Is it pretty bad for food here?" I ask.

"Yes, there's not much. Do you get enough out there?"

I smile and point to the things I have brought. "Not always quite as much as that, of course. But we get along fairly well."

My sister takes away the food. Suddenly, my mother grabs hold of my hand. She asks, "Was it very bad out there, Paul?"

Mother, what should I answer to that! You would not understand. You could never realize it. I shake my head and say, "No, Mother, not so very. There are always a lot of us together so it isn't so bad."

"Yes, but Heinrich Bredemeyer was here lately. He said it was terrible out there now, with the gas and all the rest of it."

"No, Mother, that's only talk," I say. "There's not very much in what Bredemeyer says. You see for instance, I'm well and fit—"

Before my mother's state of worry, I regain my control. Now I can walk about and answer questions without fear of having to suddenly lean against the wall.

My mother wants to get up. So I go to my sister in the kitchen. "What is the matter with her?" I ask.

She shrugs her shoulders. "She has been in bed for

some months now. We did not want to write and tell
you. Several doctors have been to see her. One of them
said it is probably cancer again."

It is pleasant to sit quietly somewhere, in the beer
garden for example. The leaves fall down on the table
and on the ground. There are no bugles and no bombardments. The children of the house play in the alley.
The sky is blue, and between the leaves of the chest-
nuts rises the green spire of the church.

This is good. I like it. But I cannot get on with the
people. My mother is the only one who asks no questions. Not so my father. He wants me to tell him about
the front. He is curious in a way that I find stupid and
upsetting. I no longer have any real contact with him.
There is nothing he likes more than hearing about it.

I realize that he does not know that a man cannot
talk of such things. I would do it willingly, but it is too
dangerous for me to put these things into words. I am
afraid that they might become too big. Then I would no
longer be able to master them. What would become of
us if everything that happens out there were quite
clear to us?

So I tell him a few amusing things. But he wants to
know whether I have ever had a hand-to-hand fight. I
say, "No," and get up and go out.

Out on the street, somebody taps me on the shoulder. It is my German teacher. He starts in with the
usual question: "Well, how are things out there?
Terrible, terrible, eh? Yes, it is awful. But we must
carry on. And after all, you do at least get decent food
out there, so I hear. You look well, Paul, and fit.
Naturally it's worse here. Naturally. The best for our
soldiers every time. That goes without saying."

He drags me along to a table with a lot of others.

They welcome me, and a head-master shakes hands with me. "So you come from the front?" he says. "What is the spirit like out there? Excellent, eh? Excellent?"

I explain that no one would be sorry to be back.

He laughs loudly. "I can well believe it! But first you have to give the Froggies[3] a good hiding. Do you smoke? Here, try one."

Unfortunately, I have accepted the cigar. So I have to stay. And they are so dripping with good will that it is impossible to object. All the same I feel annoyed. The group argue about what we should annex.[4] The head-master wants to have at least the whole of Belgium, the coal areas of France, and a slice of Russia. Then he begins to state just where in France the break-through should come.

I reply that a break-through might not be possible. The enemy may have too many reserves. Besides, the war may be rather different from what people think.

He dismisses the idea and informs me that I know nothing about it. "The details, yes," he says. "But this relates to the whole. And of that you are not able to judge. You see only your little area. So you cannot have any general idea. You do your duty, you risk your lives. That deserves the highest honor. Every man should have the Iron Cross.[5] But first of all, the enemy line must be broken through. They must be completely rolled up, from top to bottom. And then to Paris."

A moment later, I break away. He stuffs a few more cigars into my pocket. Then he sends me off with a friendly slap. "All the best! I hope we will soon hear something worthwhile from you."

---

3. **Froggies** a slang nickname for the French
4. **annex** take over
5. **Iron Cross** a German medal awarded for bravery

On the walls of my room are pinned countless pictures that I once used to cut out of the newspapers. Against the wall stand the bookshelves with my books, bought gradually with money I earned from coaching.

I want to think myself back into that time. I want to feel the same quick joy in the world of thought. It shall bring back the lost eagerness of my youth. I sit and wait.

A terrible feeling of foreignness suddenly rises up in me. I cannot find my way back. I am shut out though I put forth all my strength.

Wearily, I stand and look out the window. Then I take one of the books, intending to read. But then I put it away and take out another. I look, turn over the pages, take up fresh books. Speedily, more join the heap. Books, magazines, letters.

Words, words, words. They do not reach me.

Slowly, I place the books back on the shelves.

Quietly, I go out of the room.

I go over to see Mittelstaedt in the barracks in town. We were classmates, and now he has been promoted to company commander. He has some news for me that thrills me on the spot. He tells me that Kantorek has been called up as an ordinary soldier.

"Just think of it," says he. "I come back here from the hospital and bump right into him. He sticks out his paw and squeals, 'Hello, Mittelstaedt, how are you?' I look at him and say, 'Kantorek, business is business. Stand to attention when you speak to a superior officer.' You should have seen his face!

"He tried once again to chum up. So I snubbed him a bit harder. Then I said, 'Dismiss. You will hear from me later.' It was easy to get put in charge of his company. First thing I did was to take him to the stores and fit him out with suitable equipment. You will see in a minute."

We go to the parade ground. The company has fallen in. Mittelstaedt stands them at ease and inspects.

Then I see Kantorek and am hardly able to hold my laughter. He is wearing a faded blue tunic. On the back and in the sleeves there are big dark patches. The tunic must have belonged to a giant. The black, worn pants are much too short. They reach barely down his calf. The boots are much too big for him. And the dirty cap is too small. The whole outfit is pitiful.

Mittelstaedt stops in front of him. "Kantorek, do you call those buttons polished? You seem as though you can never learn. Inadequate, Kantorek, quite inadequate—"

It makes me bubble with glee. In school, Kantorek used to scold Mittelstaedt with exactly the same expression. "Inadequate, Mittelstaedt, quite inadequate."

Mittelstaedt continues to give him a rough time. "Look at Boettcher. Now, there's a model for you to learn from."

I can hardly believe my eyes. Boettcher is there, too. Boettcher, our school janitor. And he is a model. Kantorek shoots a glance at me as if he would like to eat me. But I grin at him innocently, as though I do not recognize him any more.

Kantorek can hardly expect anything else from Mittelstaedt. Kantorek once messed up Mittelstaedt's chance of promotion. He would be a big fool not to make the best of such a good opportunity before he goes back to the front. A man might die easier after the army has given him just one such stroke of luck.

Later, after Mittelstaedt dismisses them, I say, "Excellent. But hasn't he reported you yet?"

"He did try. Our commanding officer laughed like crazy when he heard the story. He hasn't any time for schoolmasters."

What is leave? It is a pause that only makes everything after it so much worse. Already the sense of parting has started. My mother watches me silently. I know she counts the days. Every morning, she is sad. It is one day less. She has put away my pack. She does not want to be reminded by it.

The days grow ever more strained. My mother's eyes grow more sorrowful. Four days left now. I must go and see Kemmerich's mother.

This quaking, sobbing woman shakes me and cries out to me. "Why are you living then, when he is dead?" She drowns me in tears and drops into a chair. "Did you see him then? How did he die?"

I tell her he was shot through the heart and died at once. She looks at me and doubts me. "You lie. I know better. I have felt how terribly he died. I have heard his voice at night. I have felt his pain. Tell the truth, I must know it."

"No, I was beside him. He died at once."

She pleads with me gently. "Tell me. You must tell me. I know you want to comfort me. But don't you see? It's worse for me if you don't tell me the truth. I cannot bear not knowing the truth. Tell me how it was."

I will never tell her. She can make mincemeat out of me first. I pity her. But she strikes me as rather stupid all the same. Why doesn't she stop worrying? Kemmerich will stay dead whether she knows about it or not. When a man has seen so many dead, he no longer worries about a single man. I have lost my patience. So I say, "He died at once. He felt nothing at all. His face was quite calm."

She is silent. Then says slowly, "Will you swear it?"
"Yes."

"By everything that is sacred to you?"

Good God, what is there that is sacred to me?

"Yes, he died at once."

"Are you willing never to come back yourself, if it isn't true?"

"May I never come back if he wasn't killed at once."

I would swear to anything. But she seems to believe me. She moans and weeps steadily. I have to tell how it happened, so I invent a story. I almost believe it myself.

As I leave she kisses me. The she gives me a picture of him in his recruit's uniform.

It is the last evening at home. Everyone is silent. I go to bed early. I grab the pillow, press it against myself, and bury my head in it. Who knows if I will ever lie in a feather bed again?

Late in the night, my mother comes into my room. She thinks I am asleep, and I pretend to be. To talk, to stay awake with one another, it is too hard.

She sits long into the night although she is in pain. At last, I can stand it no longer. I pretend I have just awakened.

"Go and sleep, Mother. You will catch cold here."

"I can sleep enough later," she says.

I sit up. "I don't go straight back to the front, Mother. I have to do four weeks at the training camp. I may come over from there on Sunday, perhaps."

She is silent. Then she asks gently, "Are you very much afraid?"

"No Mother."

"I would like to tell you to be on your guard against the women in France. They are no good."

Ah! Mother, Mother! You still think I am a child. Why can I not put my head in your lap and weep? Why have I always to be strong and self-controlled? Indeed, I am little more than a child. In the closet still hang short, boy's trousers. It is such a little time ago. Why is it over?

"And be very careful at the front, Paul."

Ah, Mother, Mother! Why do I not take you in my arms and die with you? What poor wretches we are!

"Yes, Mother, I will."

"I will pray for you every day, Paul." She sighs. Her face is a white gleam in the darkness.

"Now you must go to sleep, Mother."

She does not reply. And so I take her to her room. She supports herself on my arm. She is in pain. I stay with her a little while.

"And you must get well again, Mother, before I come back."

"Yes, yes, my child."

"Good night, Mother."

"Good night, my child."

The room is dark. I hear my mother's breathing and the ticking of the clock. Outside the window, the wind blows and the chestnut trees rustle.

I go back to my room. I bite into my pillow. I grasp the iron rods of my bed with my fists. I should never have come here. Out there, I did not care and was often without hope. I will never be able to be so again. I was a soldier. Now I am nothing but an agony for myself, for my mother, for everything.

I should never have come home on leave.

Chapter 8

I already know the camp on the moors.[1] But now I know hardly anyone here. As ever, all is changed. There are only a few people that I have met before.

I go through the routine without thinking. In the evenings, I generally go to the Soldiers' Home, where the newspapers are laid out. But I do not read them. Still there is a piano there that I am glad enough to play on.

The camp is surrounded with high barbed-wire fences. If we come back late from the Soldiers' Home, we have to show passes. But those who are on good terms with the guard can get through, of course.

Along the trees on the moor, we drill each day. It is bearable if one expects nothing better. The woods are beautiful with their line of birch trees. It is when one is alone that one begins to see Nature and to love her. And here I have not had much companionship. I do not even wish for it. We do not know each other very well. We only joke a bit and play poker or nap in the evenings.

Alongside our camp is the big Russian prison camp. It is separated from us by a wire fence. But in spite of this, the prisoners come across to us. They seem nervous and afraid, though most of them are big fellows with beards.

They sneak about our camp and pick over the garbage tins. One can imagine what they find there. With us food is pretty scarce and none too good at that. We get turnips cut into six pieces and boiled in water.

---

1. **moors** wide spaces of open land

They also serve us unwashed carrot tops and moldy potatoes. The one luxury is a thin rice soup with tiny bits of beef in it.

Everything gets eaten, though. If anyone doesn't want his share, there are dozens standing by ready to relieve him of it. Only the worst bits are tipped out and thrown into the garbage tins. Along with that there sometimes go a few turnip peelings, old bread crusts, and all kinds of muck.

This thin, awful garbage is what the prisoners seek. They pick it out of the stinking tins and go off with it under their shirts.

It is strange to see these enemies of ours so close up. They have faces that make one think. They have honest peasant faces, broad foreheads, broad mouths, and thick hair. They look just as kindly as our own peasants.

It is upsetting to see them begging for something to eat. They are all rather weak, for they only get enough food to keep them from starving. We ourselves have not had enough food to eat for a long time. Their backs and necks are bent, and their knees sag. Their heads hang as they beg in the few German words they know. Some men give them a kick so they fall over. Most of the men just ignore them.

I am often on guard over the Russians. They come close up to the wire fence and lean their faces against it. Their fingers hook around the mesh. They rarely speak, and then only a few words. They are more brotherly toward one another, it seems to me, than we are. But perhaps that is merely because they feel they are more unlucky than us. Anyway, the war is over so far as they are concerned.

A word of command has made these silent figures our enemies. A word of command might change them into our friends. Any non-commissioned officer is more of an enemy to a recruit then they are to us. And yet we would shoot at them again and they at us if they were free.

The days go by. On a foggy morning, another of the Russians is buried. Almost every day, one of them dies. I am on guard during the burial. The prisoners sing in parts. It sounds as if there are no voices, only an organ far away on the moor.

The burial is quickly over.

In the evening, they stand again at the wire fence. The wind comes down to them from the beech woods. The stars are cold.

Because I have already had a long leave, I get none on Sundays. So the last Sunday before I go back to the front, my father and sister come over to see me. All day, we sit in the Soldiers' Home. Where else could we go? We don't want to stay in the camp. About midday, we go for a walk on the moors.

We do not know what to talk about. So we talk about my mother's illness. It is now definitely cancer. She is already in the hospital and will be operated on shortly. The doctors hope she will recover. But we have never heard of cancer being cured.

"Where is she then?" I ask.

"In the Luisa Hospital," my father says.

"In which class?"

"Third. We must wait until we know what the operation costs. She wanted to be in the third class herself. She said that then she would have some company. And besides it is cheaper."

"So she is lying there with all those people. If only she could sleep properly."

My father nods. His face is full of worry. My mother

has always been sickly. Her illnesses have cost a great deal. My father's life has been practically given up to it.

"If only I knew how much the operation costs," he says.

"Haven't you asked?"

"Not directly. I cannot do that. The surgeon might take it the wrong way. And that would not do. He must operate on Mother."

Yes, I think bitterly, that's how it is with us. That's how it is with all poor people. They don't dare ask the price. But they worry themselves sick about it. The others, for whom it is not important, settle the price first, as a matter of course.

"The dressings afterwards are so expensive," my father says.

"Have you any money at all?"

He shakes his head. "No, but I can do some overtime."

I know. He will stand at his desk folding and pasting and cutting until 12 o'clock at night. At eight o'clock in the evening, he will eat some rubbish they get in exchange for their food tickets. Then he will take something for his headache and work on.

To cheer him up, I tell him a few stories, soldiers' jokes and the like. Afterwards, I walk with them to the railway station. They give me a pot of jam and a bag of potato-cakes my mother has made for me. Then they go off and I return to camp.

In the evening, I spread the jam on the cakes and eat some. But I have no taste for them. So I go out to give them to the Russians. Then it occurs to me that my mother cooked them herself. She was probably in pain as she stood before the stove. I put the bag back in my pack and take only two to the Russians.

Chapter 9

I search for my regiment. No one knows exactly where it lies. I hear we have become one of the flying divisions. They are pushed in wherever it is hottest. That does not sound cheerful to me. They tell me of heavy losses that we have been having. I ask about Kat and Albert. No one knows anything about them. I search farther and wander about here and there. Then at last I get some definite information. By the afternoon, I am able to report to the Orderly Room.

The sergeant-major keeps me there. The company comes back in two days. There is no reason in sending me up now.

I loaf around until the company comes back in the early morning. The men are gray, dirty, soured, and gloomy. Then I jump up and push in among them, my eyes searching. There is Tjaden, there is Müller blowing his nose, and there are Kat and Kropp. We arrange our sacks of straw side by side. I have an uneasy mind when I look at them, yet without good reason. Before we turn in, I bring out the rest of the potato-cakes and jam so they can have some too.

I could almost weep. I can hardly control myself any longer. But it will soon be all right again back here with Kat and Albert. This is where I belong.

"You've been lucky," Kropp whispers to me before we drop off to sleep. "They say we are going to Russia."

To Russia? It's not much of a war over there.

In the distance, the front thunders. The walls of the hut rattle.

There is a great deal of polishing being done. We

are inspected at every turn. Everything that is torn is exchanged for new. A rumor of peace is going around. But the other story is more likely—that we are bound for Russia. Still, what do we need new things for in Russia? At last it leaks out—the Kaiser[1] is coming to review us. That's why we've had all the inspections.

For eight whole days, one would think we were in a base-camp. There is so much drill and fuss that everyone is annoyed. At last the moment arrives. We stand to attention, and the Kaiser appears. We are curious to see what he looks like. He stalks along the line, and I am rather disappointed. Judging from his pictures, I imagined him to be bigger and more powerfully built. Above all, I expected him to have a thundering voice.

He hands out Iron Crosses, speaks to this man and that. Then we march off.

Afterwards we discuss it. Tjaden says with some shock, "So that is the All-Highest! And everyone, bar nobody, has to stand up stiff in front of him!"

"Sure," says Kat.

Then Kropp puts in. "What I would like to know is whether there would have been a war if the Kaiser had said No."

"I'm sure there would have," I say. "He was against it from the first."

"Well, if him not alone, then perhaps if 20 or 30 people in the world had said No."

"That's probable," I agree. "But they damned well said Yes."

"It's odd, when one thinks about it," Kropp goes on. "We are here to protect our fatherland. And the French are over there to protect their fatherland. Now who's in the right?"

---

1. Kaiser the leader of Germany during World War I

"Perhaps both," say I without believing it.

"Yes, well now," Albert continues. "But our professors and newspapers say that we are the only ones that are right. And let's hope so. But the French professors and newspapers say that the right is on their side. Now what about that?"

"That I don't know," I say. "But whichever way it is, there's war all the same. And every month more countries coming in."

Tjaden wonders just how a war gets started.

"Mostly by one country badly offending another," Albert answers.

Then Tjaden pretends to be stupid. "A country? I don't follow. A mountain in Germany cannot offend a mountain in France. Or a river, or a wood."

"Are you really as stupid as that?" Kropp growls. "I don't mean that at all. One people offends the other—"

"Then I haven't any business here at all," Tjaden replies. "I don't feel myself offended."

"Well, it doesn't apply to tramps like you," Albert says sourly.

"Then I can be going home right away," Tjaden says, and we all laugh.

"Ach, man! He means the people as a whole, the State—" exclaims Müller.

"True," Kat says. "But just you consider, almost all of us are simple folk. And in France, too, the majority of the men are laborers, workmen, or poor clerks. Now just why would a French blacksmith or a French shoemaker want to attack us? No, it is merely the rulers. I had never seen a Frenchman before I came here. And it will be just the same with the majority of Frenchmen. They weren't asked about it any more than we were."

"Then what exactly is the war for?" Tjaden asks.

Kat shrugs his shoulders. "There must be some people to whom the war is useful."

"Well, I'm not one of them," Tjaden grins.

"Not you, nor anybody else here."

"Who are they then?" asks Tjaden. "It isn't any use to the Kaiser. He has everything he can want."

"I'm not so sure about that," Kat says. "He has not had a war up till now. And every full-grown emperor needs at least one war. Otherwise he would not become famous. You look in your school books."

"And generals, too," Detering adds. "They become famous through war."

"Even more famous than emperors," Kat says.

"There are other people back behind there who prof it by the war, that's for sure," growls Detering.

"I think it is more of a kind of fever," Albert says. "No one in particular wants it. And then all at once, there it is. We didn't want the war. The others say the same thing. And yet half the world is in it all the same."

Müller gets up. "Anyway, it is better that the war is here instead of in Germany. Just you look at the shell-holes."

"True," Tjaden says. "But no war at all would be better still."

Albert lies down on the grass. He growls angrily, "The best thing is not to talk about the rotten business."

"It won't make any difference, that's sure," agrees Kat.

To make matters worse, we have to return all the new things and take back our old rags again. The good ones were just for the inspection.

Instead of going to Russia, we go up the line again.

On the way, we pass through a wood with the tree trunks shattered and the ground plowed up.

At several places there are huge craters. "Great guns, something has hit that," I say to Kat.

"Trench mortars," he replies. Then he points up at one of the trees.

In the branches, dead men are hanging. A naked soldier is squatting in the fork of a tree. He still has his helmet on. Otherwise, he is entirely without clothes. There is only half of him sitting up there, the top half. The legs are missing.

"What can that mean?" I ask.

"He's been blown out of his clothes," mutters Tjaden.

"It's funny," Kat says. "We have seen that several times now. If a mortar gets you, it blows you clean out of your clothes."

I search around. And so it is. Here hang bits of uniform. Somewhere else is plastered a bloody mess that was once a human limb. Over there lies a body with nothing but a piece of underpants on one leg and the collar of the tunic around its neck. Otherwise, it is naked. The clothes are hanging up in the tree. Both arms are missing as though they had been pulled out. I discover one of them 20 yards off in a shrub.

"That's no joke, Kat," I say.

"No more than a shell splinter in the belly," he replies, shrugging his shoulders.

All of this can only have happened a little while ago. The blood is still fresh. Everybody we see there is dead. We do not waste any more time. We report the affair at the next stretcher-bearer's post. After all, it is not our business to take these stretcher-bearers' jobs away from them.

A patrol has to be sent out to discover just how strongly the enemy position is manned. Since my leave, I feel a certain strong attachment to the other fellows. So I volunteer to go with them. We slip out through the wire and then divide and creep forward separately. After a while, I find a shallow shell-hole and crawl into it. From here, I peer forward.

There is moderate machine-gun fire. It sweeps across from all directions. It's not very heavy but enough to make one keep down.

A bomb or something lands close beside me. I have not heard it coming and am terrified. I try to pull myself together. It is not my first patrol and not a very risky one. But it is the first one since my leave. And besides, the lie of the land is still rather strange to me.

I am panting softly. I have a simple animal fear of poking out my head.

I hear muffled voices. A new warmth flows through me. They are more than life to me, these voices. They are the voices of my comrades.

Cautiously, I glide out over the edge and snake my way forward. I advance a long way and then turn back in a wide curve. I have not established touch with the others. Every yard nearer our trench fills me with confidence—and with haste, too. It would be bad to get hit right now.

Then a new fear lays hold of me. I can no longer remember the direction. Quiet, I squat in a shell-hole and try to locate myself. More than once, it has happened that some fellow has jumped into a trench only then to discover that it was the wrong one.

A shell crashes. Almost immediately, two others. And then it begins for real. A bombardment. Machine-guns rattle. Now there is nothing for it but to stay lying low. Apparently an attack is coming. Everywhere the rockets shoot up.

I lie still. Somewhere, something clanks, stamps, and stumbles over. All my nerves become tight. It clatters over me and away. The first wave has passed. I have but one thought: What will you do if someone jumps into your shell-hole? Swiftly, I pull out my little dagger. I grasp it and bury it in my hand under the mud. If anyone jumps in here I will go for him. I shall stab him clean through the throat so that he shall not call out. That's the only way.

Now our batteries are firing. A shell lands near me. That makes me savage with fury. All it needs now is to be killed by our own shells. I curse and grind my teeth in the mud. It is madness. All I can do is groan and pray.

Already it has become somewhat lighter. Steps hasten over me. The rattle of machine-guns becomes an unbroken chain. Just as I am about to turn around a little, something heavy stumbles. With a crash, a body falls over me into the shell-hole, and lies across me.

I do not think at all. I strike madly. I feel the body tighten and then become limp. When I recover, my hand is sticky and wet.

The man gurgles. I want to stop his mouth, stuff it with earth. He must be quiet. He is betraying me. But I have suddenly become so weak that I cannot lift my hand against him.

So I crawl away to the farthest corner and stay there. My hand grasps the knife—ready, if he stirs, to spring at him again. But he won't do so any more. I can hear that already in his gurgling.

I have but one desire—to get away. If it is not soon, it will be too light. Then, as I try to raise up my head, I see it is impossible already. The machine-gun fire so sweeps the ground that I should be shot through before I could make one jump.

Then I notice my bloody hand and suddenly feel sick. I take some earth and rub the skin with it. Now my hand is muddy and the blood cannot be seen any more.

The fire does not stop. It is equally heavy from both sides. Our fellows have probably given me up for lost long ago.

It is early morning, clear gray. The figure opposite me moves. I look at it. A man with a small pointed beard lies there. His head is fallen to one side. One arm is half-bent. His head rests helplessly upon it. The other hand lies on his chest. It is bloody.

I drag myself toward him. I support myself on my hands, creep a bit farther and wait. At last, I am beside him.

Then he opens his eyes. He must have heard me. He gazes at me with a look of utter terror. The body is perfectly still, but the eyes cry out. All the life is gathered in them for one great effort to flee.

My legs give way, and I drop on my elbows. "No, no," I whisper. I raise one hand. I must show him that I want to help him. I stroke his forehead.

I give him some water. He gulps it down. Then I unbutton his tunic to bandage him if it is possible. In any case, I must do it. If the fellows over there capture me they will see that I wanted to help him. So they will not shoot me. The shirt is stuck and will not come away. I must cut it open.

There are three stabs. My field dressing covers them. The blood runs out under it. I press it tighter. He groans.

That's all I can do. Now we must wait, wait.

The gurgling starts again. How slowly a man dies! For this I know—he cannot be saved. I have tried to tell myself that he will be. At noon, this pretense breaks down and melts before his groans.

This is the first time I have killed with my hands, someone close at hand, whose death is my doing. Every gasp lays my heart bare. I would give much if he would but stay alive. It is hard to lie here and to have to see and hear him.

In the afternoon, about three, he is dead.

I breathe freely again. But only for a short time. Soon the silence is more horrible than the groans.

It is mad what I do. But I must do something. I prop the dead man up again so that he lies comfortably, although he feels nothing any more. I close his eyes. They are brown. His hair is black and a bit curly at the sides.

The silence spreads. I talk and must talk. So I speak to him. "Comrade, I did not want to kill you. If you jumped in here again, I would not do it. But you were only an idea to me before. You were an idea that lived in my mind and called forth the proper response. But now, for the first time, I see you are a man like me. Forgive me, comrade.

"I will write to your wife," I say to the dead man. "She must hear it from me. I will tell her everything. She shall not suffer. I will help her, and your parents too, and your child—"

His tunic is half-open. The pocket book is easy to find. In it is the book with his name. I hesitate. So long as I do not know his name, perhaps I may still forget him. Time will erase this picture. But his name is a nail that will be hammered into me and never come out.

I take the wallet in my hand. It slips and falls open.

Some pictures and letters drop out. There are portraits of a woman and a little girl. I take the letters and try to read them. Most of it I do not understand. Each word I can translate from French stabs me in the chest.

My brain is taxed to the limit. But I realize this much. I will never write to these people as I intended. Impossible. I look at the pictures once more. They are clearly not rich people. I might send them money later, without letting on who I am. This dead man is bound up with my life. Therefore I must do everything, promise everything to save myself. I swear blindly that I mean to live only for his sake and his family. So I open the book and read slowly—Gérard Duval, printer.

With the dead man's pencil I write the address on an envelope. Then I quickly push everything back into the tunic.

I have killed the printer, Gérard Duval. I must be a printer, I think in confusion. Be a printer—a printer—

By afternoon I am calmer. My fear was groundless. The name troubles me no more. The madness passes. "Comrade," I say to the dead man, "today you, tomorrow me. But if I come out of it, comrade, I will fight against this, that has struck us both down. I promise you, comrade. It shall never happen again."

The sun strikes low. I am exhausted and hungry. I fall into a doze and do not at first realize that evening is approaching. The darkness grows. I wait until the first rocket goes up. Then I crawl out of the shell-hole. I fix my eyes on another shell-hole. I scurry over to it. Then I grope farther, spring into the next, scramble onward.

I come nearer. By the light of the rocket, I see something move in the wire. I am suspicious until I recognize our helmets. Then I call. Right away an answer rings out, my name: "Paul—"

I call again in answer. It is Kat and Albert. They have come out with a stretcher to look for me.

"Are you wounded?"

"No, no—"

We drop into the trench. I ask for something to eat and wolf it down. In a few words, I tell what happened. There is nothing new about it. It happens quite often.

I do not mention the dead printer.

By next morning, I can keep it to myself no longer. I must tell Kat and Albert. They both try to calm me. "You can't do anything about it. What else could you have done? That is what you are here for."

I listen to them and feel comforted. It was just nonsense that I talked out there in the shell-hole.

"Look there for instance," points Kat.

On the fire-step stand some snipers. They rest their rifles with telescopic sights on the parapet and watch the enemy front. Once and again, a shot cracks out.

Then we hear a cry, "That's found a home! Did you see how he leapt in the air?" Sergeant Oellrich turns around proudly and scores his point. He heads the list today with three hits.

"What do you say to that?" Kat asks.

I nod. We look at one another. "I would not do it," I say.

"All the same, it's very good for you to see it just now," says Kat.

"You don't need to lose any sleep over your affair," nods Albert.

And now I hardly understand it myself any more.

"It was only because I had to lie with him so long," I say. "After all, war is war."

Oellrich's rifle cracks out sharply and dry.

Chapter 10

We have dropped in for a good job. Eight of us have to guard a village that has been abandoned. It is being shelled too heavily.

We have to watch the supply dump. We are supposed to get provisions for ourselves from the same store. We are just the right people for that. Kat, Albert, Müller, Tjaden, Detering; our whole gang is there. Haie is dead, though. But we are mighty lucky all the same. All the other squads have had more losses than we have.

We select a dug-out. It is a concrete cellar into which steps lead down from above. The entrance is protected by a separate concrete wall.

The floor is first covered with mattresses that we haul in from the houses. Only in the middle of the floor is there any clear space. Then we bring in blankets and quilts, wonderful soft affairs. There is plenty of everything to be had in the village. Albert and I find a beautiful wooden bed. We sweat like monkeys moving it in. But a man cannot let a thing like that go by. And it certainly would be shot to pieces in a day or two.

Kat and I do a little patrolling through the houses. In very short time, we have collected a dozen eggs and two pounds of fairly fresh butter. Suddenly, there is a crash in the living room. An iron stove hurtles through the wall past us and on through the wall behind. Two holes. It comes from the house opposite where a shell has just landed. "The swine," Kat says angrily. We continue our search.

All at once, we prick up our ears, hurry across, and suddenly stand frozen. There running up and down in a little sty are two live pigs. We rub our eyes and look once again to make certain. Yes, they are still there. We grab hold of them.

This will make a grand feed. About 20 yards from our dug-out, there is a small house that was used as an officers' billet. In the kitchen is a huge fireplace with two ranges, pots, pans, and kettles. There is everything one could need—even a stack of small chopped wood.

Two of our fellows have been out in the fields all morning. They've been hunting for potatoes, carrots, and green peas. We sniff at the tinned stuff in the supply dump. We want fresh vegetables. In the dining-room, there are already two heads of cauliflower.

The pigs are slaughtered. Kat sees to them. We want to make potato-cakes to go with the roast. Kat takes charge of the pigs, the carrots, the peas, and the cauliflower. I fry the pancakes, four at a time. The pigs are roasted whole. We all stand around them as before an altar.

Then we begin to realize we are in for trouble. They have spotted the smoke from our chimney. The shells start to drop on us. They keep dropping closer and closer all around us. Still we cannot just leave all the food.

At last, everything is ready. We organize the moving of it back to the dug-out. After the next explosion, two men dash across the 50 yards to the dug-out with the pots of vegetables. We see them disappear.

The next shot. Everyone ducks, and then two more trot off. They each have a big can of the finest coffee. They reach the dug-out before the next explosion.

Then Kat and Kropp grab the masterpiece—the big dish with the brown, roasted pigs. Away they race.

I stay to finish my last four pancakes. Twice I have to drop to the floor. After all, it means four pancakes more, and they are my favorite dish.

Then I grab the plate with the great pile of cakes and squeeze myself behind the house door. I gallop off with the plate clamped against my chest with both hands. I run like a deer and sweep around the wall. Fragments clatter against the concrete. I tumble down the cellar steps. My elbows are skinned, but I have not lost a single pancake.

At two o'clock, we start the meal. It lasts until six. We drink coffee until half-past six, officers' coffee from the supply dump. Exactly at half-past six, we begin supper. At ten o'clock, we throw the bones of the pigs outside the door. Then there is brandy and rum—also from the supply dump.

Almost two weeks pass this way in eating, drinking, and roaming about. No one disturbs us. The village gradually vanishes under the shells, and we lead a charmed life. So long as any part of the supply dump still stands, we don't worry. We wish nothing better than to stay here until the end of the war.

After eight more days, we receive orders to go back. The palmy days are over. Two big motor trucks take us away. Still, we stow a bag full of the choicest things to eat. We often dip into it. The tough ham sausages, the tins of liver sausages, and the boxes of cigarettes rejoice our hearts. Each man has a bag to himself.

Slowly, the trucks roll down the road. We sing. Behind us, shells are sending up fountains from the now utterly abandoned village.

A few days later, we are sent to evacuate a village. On the way, we meet the fleeing residents. They carry their goods and possessions with them in wheelbarrows and on their backs. Their figures are bent. Their faces are full of grief and fear. The children hold on to their mothers' hands. A few carry miserable-looking dolls. All are silent as they pass us by.

We are marching in column. The French certainly will not fire on a town in which there are still residents. But a few minutes later, the air screams and cries ring out. A shell has landed among our rear guard. We scatter and fling ourselves down on the ground. The next moment, a blow sweeps like a whip over my left leg. I hear Albert cry out. He is beside me.

"Where has it got you?" I ask.

"In the knee, I think."

"Can you run?"

"I think—"

"Then let's go," I yell, for we are lying uncovered in the open field.

He staggers up and runs. I keep next to him. We make for the ditch beside the road and run along it. The shelling follows us. The road leads toward the munition dump. If that goes up, there won't be so much as a bootlace left of us. So we change our plan and run diagonally across country.

Albert begins to drag. "You go. I'll come on after," he says, and throws himself down.

I grab him by the arm and shake him. "Up, Albert. If you lie down once, you'll never get any farther. Quick, I'll hold you up."

At last, we reach a small dug-out. Kropp pitches in, and I bandage him up. The shot is just a little above the knee. Then I take a look at myself. My pants are bloody and my arm, too. Albert binds up my wound with his field dressing. Already he is no longer able to move his leg. We both wonder how we managed to get this far. Fear alone made it possible. We would have run even if our feet had been cut off. We would have run on the stumps.

I can still crawl a little. I call out to a passing ambulance that picks us up. It is full of wounded. An army medical officer sticks an anti-tetanus needle into our chests.

At the dressing station, we lie side by side.

"Now for home, Albert," I say.

"Let's hope so," he replies. "I only wish I knew what I've got. How far above the knee am I hit?"

"At least four inches, Albert," I answer. Actually, it is perhaps one.

"I've made up my mind," he says after a while. "If they take my leg, I'll put an end to it. I won't go through life as a cripple."

So we lie there with our thoughts and wait.

In the evening, we are hauled on to the chopping-block. I am frightened and think quickly what I should do. Everyone knows that the surgeons in the dressing stations amputate for the slightest reason. It is much simpler than complicated patching. I think of Kemmerich. Whatever happens I will not let them chloroform[1] me, even if I have to crack a few of their skulls.

The surgeon pokes around in my wound and a blackness comes before my eyes. "Don't carry on so," he says gruffly. The pain is terrible. Two orderlies hold my arms down. But I break loose and try to crash into the doctor's glasses. "Put him under," he roars madly.

Then I become quiet. "Pardon me, Herr Doctor. I will keep still. But do not chloroform me."

"Well, now," he says. He takes up his instruments again. He is a fair fellow, not more than 30 years old.

---

1. **chloroform**   a gas used to anesthetize, or make unconscious

Now I see that he is tormenting me. He is merely raking about in the wound and looking up at me over his glasses. My hands squeeze around the grips. I'll kick the bucket before he will get a squeak out of me.

He has fished out a piece of shell and tosses it to me. He appears pleased at my self-control. Now he sets my leg carefully in splints. Then he says, "Tomorrow you'll be off home." Then I am put in plaster. Soon I am back again with Kropp. I tell him that a hospital train comes in tomorrow morning.

"We must work the army medical sergeant-major so that we can keep together, Albert."

I manage to slip the sergeant-major two of my cigars. Then I tip the word to him. He smells the cigars. "Have you got any more of them?" he asks.

"Another good handful," I say. "And my comrade," I point to Kropp, "has some as well. We might be glad to hand them to you out of the window of the hospital train in the morning."

He understands, of course. He smells them once again and says, "Done."

Our stretchers stand on the platform. We wait for the train. It rains and the station has no roof. Our blankets are thin. We have waited already two hours.

The stretchers are sopping wet by the time the train arrives. The sergeant-major sees to it that we are put in the same car. There is a crowd of Red Cross nurses. Kropp is stowed in below. I am lifted up and told to get into the bed above him.

"Good God!" I cry out.

"What is it?" asks the sister.

I cast a glance at the bed. It is covered with clean snow-white linen. And my shirt has gone six weeks without being washed and is terribly muddy.

"Can't you get in by yourself?" the sister asks.

"Why yes," I say in a sweat. "But take off the bed cover first."

"What for?"

I feel like a pig. Must I get in there? "It will get—"

"A little bit dirty?" she suggests helpfully. "That doesn't matter. We will wash it again afterwards."

"No, no, not that—" I say excitedly.

"What is it then?"

"Because of the lice," I bawl out at last.

She laughs. "Well, they must have a good day for once, too."

Now I don't care any more. I scramble into bed and pull up the covers.

A hand gropes over the bed cover. The sergeant-major. He goes off with the cigars.

An hour later, we notice we are moving.

The train travels slowly. Sometimes it halts and the dead are unloaded. It halts often.

The next morning, Albert is feverish. I don't feel too bad. We sleep through the days. The country glides quietly by the window. The third night, I hear from the sister that Albert is to be put off at the next station because of his fever.

"Albert," I say, "we stick together. You see."

On the sister's next round, I hold my breath and press it up into my head. My face turns red.

She stops and says, "Are you in pain?"

"Yes," I groan. "All of a sudden."

She gives me a thermometer and goes on. I stick it under my arm and flip it steadily with my forefinger. Then I shake it. I send it up to 101.6 degrees.

When the sister comes back, she notes me down on a slip of paper. I know my bandage will not be opened if it can be avoided.

Albert and I are put off together.

We are in the same room in a Catholic Hospital. That is a piece of luck. The Catholic hospitals are noted for their good treatment and good food. The hospital has been filled up from our train. There are a great many bed cases amongst them.

There are eight men in our room. Peter, a curly black-haired fellow, has the worst injury—a very bad lung wound. Franz Wachter, alongside him, has a shot in the arm. It didn't look too bad at first. But the third night, he calls out to us. He thinks he is bleeding.

I ring loudly. The night sister does not come. We have been making rather heavy demands on her during the night. We have all been freshly bandaged, and so we have a good deal of pain.

We wait. Then Franz says, "Ring again."

I do so. Still she does not come. At last the door opens. The old lady appears, mumbling. When she see Franz's trouble, she says, "Why didn't someone say I was wanted?"

"We did ring. And none of us here can walk."

He has been bleeding badly, and she binds him up. In the morning, we look at his face. It has become sharp and yellow. Now a sister comes more often.

Franz Wachter does not regain his strength. One day, he is taken away and does not come back. Josef Hamacher knows all about it. "We shall not see him again. They have put him in the Dead Room."

"What do you mean, Dead Room?" Kropp asks.

"Well, Dying Room—"

"What is that, then?"

"A little room at the corner of the building. Whoever is about to kick the bucket is put in there. There are two beds in it. It is usually called the Dying Room."

"But what do they do that for?"

"They don't have so much work to do afterward. The room is right next to the mortuary[2]. Perhaps they do it for the sake of the others also. And they can look after him better if he is by himself."

"But what about him?"

Josef shrugs his shoulders. "Usually, he doesn't take much notice anymore."

"Does everybody know about it then?"

"Anyone who has been here long enough knows."

In the afternoon, Franz Wachter's bed has a new person in it. A few days later, they take the new man away, too. We see many come and go.

Often, relatives sit by the bed and weep or talk softly. One old woman will not go away. But she cannot stay through the night. The next morning she comes very early, but not early enough. When she goes up to the bed, someone else is in it already. She has to go to the mortuary. The apples she has brought with her she gives to us.

Then little Peter begins to get worse. One day, the flat trolley stands beside his bed. "Where to?" he asks.

"To the bandaging ward."

He is lifted out. But the sister makes a mistake. She removes his tunic from the hook and puts it on the trolley, too. Peter understands right away. He tries to roll off the trolley. They push him back. "I won't go to the Dying Room," he cries out fiercely.

"But we are going to the bandaging ward."

"Then what do you want my tunic for?"

They do not answer but wheel him out. At the door,

---

2. **mortuary** a place where dead bodies are brought

he tries to raise himself up. His eyes are full of tears. "I will come back again! I will come back again!" he cries.

The door shuts. We are all excited, but we say nothing. At last Josef says, "Many a man has said that. Once a man is in there, he never comes through."

I am operated on and vomit for two days. My bones will not grow together. Another fellow's have grown crooked. It is horrible.

It is going badly with Albert. They have taken him and amputated his leg. The whole leg has been taken off from the thigh. Now he will hardly speak any more. Once, he says he will shoot himself the first time he can get hold of his revolver again.

Again beds are empty. Day after day goes by with pain and fear, groans and death gurgles. Even the Death Room is no use any more. It is too small. Fellows die during the night in our room. They go even faster than the sisters can cope with them.

However, one day the door flies open and the flat trolley rolls in. And there on the stretcher, pale, thin, upright, and victorious sits Peter. The sister is beaming as she pushes him over to his former bed. He is back from the Dying Room. We have long supposed him dead.

He looks round. "What do you say now?"

And Josef has to admit that it is the first time he has ever known of such a thing.

Gradually, a few of us are allowed to get up. And I am given crutches to hobble around on. But I do not make much use of them. I cannot bear Albert's gaze as I move about the room. His eyes always follow me with such a strange look. So I sometimes escape to the hallway. There I can move about more freely.

A man cannot realize that above such shattered

bodies, there are still human faces. And this is only one hospital. There are hundreds of thousands in Germany, hundreds of thousands in France, hundreds of thousands in Russia. How senseless is everything that can ever be written, done, or thought when such things are possible. A hospital alone shows what war is.

I am young. I am 20 years old. Yet, I know nothing of life but despair, death, and fear. I see how peoples are set against one another. In silence, unknowingly, foolishly, obediently, they slay one another. And all my generation is experiencing these things with me. What do they expect of us if a time ever comes when the war is over? Our knowledge of life is limited to death. What shall come out of us?

After a few weeks, I have to go each morning to the massage department. There my leg is harnessed up and made to move. The arm has healed long since.

Albert's stump heals well. In a few weeks, he should go off to a place for artificial limbs. He continues not to talk much. He often breaks off in his speech and stares in front of him. If he were not here with us, he would have shot himself long ago. But now he is over the worst of it. He often looks on while we play cards.

I get health leave.

My mother does not want to let me go away. She is very weak. It is all much worse than it was last time.

Then I am recalled to my regiment. I return once more to the line.

Parting from my friend Albert Kropp was very hard. But a man gets used to that sort of thing in the army.

Chapter 11

We count the weeks no more. It was winter when I came up. When the shells exploded, the frozen clods of earth were just as dangerous as the fragments. Now the trees are green again. We have almost grown used to war. It is a cause of death, like cancer and tuberculosis. The deaths are merely more frequent, more terrible.

Men condemned to death feel a desperate loyalty to one another. Living in the midst of danger, we seek a full enjoyment of the hours as they come. For example, Tjaden spoons down his ham-and-pea soup rapidly when an enemy attack is reported. He simply cannot be sure that in an hour's time he will be alive. We have discussed it at length, whether it is right or not. Kat is against it. He says a man has to think of the possibility of a stomach wound. And that is more dangerous on a full stomach than an empty one.

Such things are real problems. They are serious matters. They cannot be otherwise. Here, on the borders of death, life follows a very simple course. It is limited to what is most necessary. All else lies buried in gloomy sleep. And at night, waking out of dream, a man sees with alarm how thin the boundary that divides him from the darkness. We are little flames poorly sheltered against the storm. We flicker and sometimes almost go out. Then the muffled roar of the battle surrounds us. Our only comfort is the breathing of our comrades asleep. And so we wait for morning.

Every day and every hour, every shell and every death cuts into this thin support. And the years waste it rapidly. I see how this support is already gradually breaking down around me.

There is the mad story of Detering.

He was one of those who kept to himself. His misfortune was that he saw a cherry tree in a garden. We were just coming back from the front line. At a turning of the road near our billets, beautiful in the morning twilight, stood this cherry tree before us. It had no leaves but was one white mass of blossom.

In the evening, Detering was not to be seen. Then at last he came back. He had a couple of branches of cherry blossoms in his hand. We made fun of him and asked whether he was going to a wedding. He made no answer but lay down on his bed. I sensed something was wrong and went over to him. He made out it was nothing. "Don't do anything silly, Detering," I said.

"Ach, why—it's merely that I can't sleep—"

"What did you pick the cherry branches for?"

"Surely I can pick cherry blossoms if I want to!" he replied. "I have a big orchard with cherry trees at home. When they are in blossom, they look like one single sheet, so white. It is just the time."

"Perhaps you will get leave soon. You may even be sent back as a farmer."

He nodded but he was far away. To turn him away from his thoughts I asked him for a piece of bread. He gave it to me without a murmur. That was suspicious, for he is usually tight-fisted. So I stayed awake. Nothing happened. In the morning, he was his usual self.

The second morning, he was gone. I noticed it but said nothing. He might perhaps get through. Various fellows have already gotten into Holland.

However, at roll call he was missed. A week after, we heard that he had been caught by the military police. He had headed toward Germany. Anyone might have known he left because he was homesick. But what does a court-martial 100 miles behind the front-line care? We have heard nothing more of Detering.

Müller is dead. Someone shot him point blank in the stomach. He lived for half an hour, quite conscious, and in terrible pain.

Before he died, he handed over his pocket-book to me. He also left me his boots—the same that he once inherited from Kemmerich. I wear them, for they fit me quite well. After me, Tjaden will get them. I have promised them to him.

We have been able to bury Müller. But he is not likely to remain undisturbed for long. Our lines are falling back. There are too many fresh English and American troops over there. There's too much corned beef and white bread. Too many guns. Too many airplanes.

We are wasting away and starved. Our food is bad. It's mixed up with so much substitute stuff that it makes us ill. The factory owners in Germany have grown wealthy; dysentery dissolves our bowels.

Our artillery is fired out. It has too few shells, and the barrels are so worn that they shoot uncertainly. They scatter so widely that they fall on ourselves. We have too few horses. Our fresh troops are weak boys in need of rest. They cannot carry a pack but merely know how to die. By the thousands. They understand nothing about warfare. They simply go on and let themselves be shot down. A single flyer mowed down two companies of them for a joke. They had just come fresh from the train.

"Germany should be empty soon," Kat says.

We have given up hope that an end may come. We never think so far. A man can stop a bullet and be killed. He can get wounded. Then the hospital is his next stop. There he will fall into the hands of one of those staff surgeons. And the doctor says to him, "What, one leg a bit short? If you have any guts, you don't need to run at the front. The man is A1.[1] Dismiss!"

Kat tells a story that has traveled the length of the front. It's a story of the staff surgeon who reads the names on the list. When a man comes before him, without looking up he says, "A1. We need soldiers up there." A fellow with a wooden leg comes up before him. The staff surgeon again says A1. "And then," Kat raises his voice, "the fellow speaks up. 'I already have a wooden leg. But when I go back again and they shoot off my head, then I will get a wooden head made and become a staff surgeon.'" This answer tickles us all greatly.

The months pass by. The summer of 1918 is the most bloody and the most terrible. Every man here knows we are losing the war. Not much is said about it. We will not be able to attack after this big offensive. We have no more men and no more ammunition.

Still the campaign goes on—the dying goes on—

Summer of 1918—Never was so much silently suffered as in the moment when we leave once again for the front. Wild rumors of an armistice[2] and peace are in the air. They lay hold on our hearts and make the return to the front harder than ever.

Summer of 1918—Never was life more bitter and full of horror than in the hours of the bombardment. When the faces lie in the dirt and the hands clutch at one thought: No! No! Not now at the last moment!

It is on one of these late summer days, while bring-

---

1. **A1** military classification that a man is fit to fight
2. **armistice** an agreement by the parties in a war to stop fighting

ing food, that Kat falls. We two are alone. I bind up his wound. His shin is smashed. It has got the bone, and Kat groans desperately. "At last—just at the last—"

I comfort him. "Who knows how long this mess will go on yet! Now you are saved—"

The wound begins to bleed fast. Kat cannot be left by himself. He is not very heavy. So I take him up on my back and start off to the dressing station with him.

Twice we rest. I sweat and my face is swollen with the strain of carrying. The going is more difficult. Often, a shell whistles across. We lie down to wait till the shelling is over. I give Kat some tea from my water bottle.

"Well, Kat, we are going to be separated at last," I say sadly.

He is silent and looks at me.

"Do you remember, Kat, how we caught and cooked the goose? And how you brought me out of the barrage when I was still a young recruit and was wounded for the first time? I cried then, Kat. That is almost three years ago."

He nods. The pain of being alone rises up in me. When Kat is gone, I will not have one friend left.

"Kat, in any case we must see one another again, if it is peace-time before you come back."

"Do you think that I will be marked A1 again with this leg?" he asks bitterly.

"With rest, it will get better. The joint is quite sound. It may get all right again. Perhaps we could do something together later on, Kat." I am miserable. It is impossible that perhaps I shall not see Kat again.

"In any case, give me your address at home, Kat. And here is mine. I will write it down for you."

I write his address in my pocket book.

Suddenly, Kat gurgles and turns green and yellow.

"Let us go on," he stammers.

I jump up, eager to help him. I take him and start off at a run. At last, we reach the dressing station.

My legs tremble. I have trouble finding my bottle to take a drink. But I smile—Kat is saved.

Soon a voice falls on my ears. "You might have spared yourself that," an orderly says.

I look at him but do not understand.

He points to Kat. "He is stone dead."

"He has been hit in the shin," I say.

The orderly stands still. "That as well."

I turn around and peer at Kat. He lies still. "Fainted," I say quickly.

The orderly says softly, "He is dead."

I shake my head. "Only ten minutes ago I was talking to him. He has fainted."

Kat's hands are warm. I pass my hand under his shoulders to rub his temples with some tea. I feel my fingers become moist. As I draw them away from his head, they are bloody. "You see," the orderly says.

On the way, without my having noticed it, Kat has caught a splinter in the head. There is just one little hole. It must have been one tiny, stray splinter. But it is enough. Kat is dead.

Slowly, I get up.

"Would you like to take his paybook and his things?" the lance-corporal asks me.

I nod and he gives them to me.

The orderly is puzzled. "Are you related?"

No, we are not related.

Do I walk? Have I feet still? I raise my eyes. I let them move around and turn myself with them one full circle. All is as usual. Only the Militiaman Stanislaus Katczinsky has died.

Then I know nothing more.

Chapter 12

It is autumn. There are not many of the old hands left. I am the last of the seven fellows from our class.

Everyone talks of peace and armistice. All wait. Hope is high. It cannot be taken away again without an uprising. If there is not peace, then there will be revolution.

I have 14 days rest because I have swallowed a bit of gas. In the little garden, I sit the whole day long in the sun. The armistice is coming soon. I believe it now, too. Then we will go home.

Here my thoughts stop and will not go any farther. All that meets me, all that floods over me are but feelings. I feel a greed for life, a love of home, a yearning for release from this madness. But I have no aims.

Had we returned home in 1916, it might have been different. Out of the suffering and the strength of our experience, we might have unleashed a storm. Now if we go back, we will be weary, broken, burnt out, and without hope. We will not be able to find our way any more.

And men will not understand us. The generation that grew up before us had a home and a calling. Now it will return to its old occupation, and the war will be forgotten. And the generation that has grown up after us will be strange to us and push us aside. The years will pass by, and in the end we shall fall into ruin.

However, perhaps all this that I think is sadness and sorrow. Perhaps it will fly away as the dust when I stand once again beneath the trees and listen to the rustling of their leaves. It cannot be that it has gone, the melodies from dreams and from books. It cannot be that this has vanished in bombardments, in despair.

I stand up.

I am very quiet. Let the months and years come. They can take nothing from me. They can take nothing more. I am so alone and so without hope that I can face them without fear. The life that has carried me through these years is still in my hands and my eyes. Whether I have subdued it, I do not know. But so long as it is there it will seek its own way out, no matter the will within me.

Paul Baümer fell in October 1918. It was a day that was quiet and still. The army report contained only a single sentence: All quiet on the Western Front.

He had fallen forward and lay on the earth as though sleeping. Turning him over, one saw that he could not have suffered long. His face had a calm look, as though he was almost glad the end had come.

REVIEWING YOUR READING

CHAPTER 1

FINDING THE MAIN IDEA

1. Paul Baümer and his classmates were persuaded to enlist in the German army by their

   (A) parents (B) local army recruiter (C) friends (D) teacher.

REMEMBERING DETAILS

2. The first of the group of classmates to die in battle was

   (A) Tjaden (B)Kantorek (C) Behm (D) Kemmerich.

DRAWING CONCLUSIONS

3. The company commander orders the cook to serve everything to the men because

   (A) he disliked the cook (B) he knew they deserved it after all they'd been through (C) he wanted to get rid of all the food at once (D) he was hungry, too.

THINKING IT OVER

4. Why do you think Paul and his friends are so bitter toward their former teacher, Kantorek, and the members of his whole generation? Explain.

CHAPTER 2

FINDING THE MAIN IDEA

1. A good title for this chapter might be

   (A) "The Loss of a Friend" (B) "A Happy Reunion" (C) "Fun in Basic Training" (D) "A Fierce Battle."

REMEMBERING DETAILS

2. Who is in charge of Paul's platoon in camp?

   (A) Kantorek (B) Katczinsky (C) Himmelstoss (D) Müller.

DRAWING CONCLUSIONS

3. Because they had a rough time in training, Paul and his friends developed a sense of

(A) happiness (B) toughness (C) humor (D) fairness.

USING YOUR REASON

4. Corporal Himmelstoss stopped picking on Paul and his friends because

    (A) Paul and Kropp stood up to him (B) he grew to like the (C) they paid him money (D) he left the army.

THINKING IT OVER

5. Paul says that because of the war, his generation has become a "waste land." What does he mean by that? Explain.

CHAPTER 3

FINDING THE MAIN IDEA

1. Katczinsky has a real talent for finding

    (A) gold (B) food (C) money (D) places to sleep.

REMEMBERING DETAILS

2. Paul and his friends are excited by the expected arrival of

    (A) a new commander (B) Kantorek (C) Himmelstoss (D) Kemmerich.

DRAWING CONCLUSIONS

3. Paul and his friends decide to "square accounts" with Himmelstoss because

    (A) he asks them to (B) they are paid to (C) they want to get into trouble (D) they are going to the front the next day.

THINKING IT OVER

4. Katczinsky's view of the war can be summed in the poem he quotes: *'Give 'em all the same grub and all the same pay/And the war would be over and done in a day.'* What do you think those lines mean?

CHAPTER 4

FINDING THE MAIN IDEA

1. This chapter is mostly about

    (A) troops riding on horseback (B) how to put on gas masks

(C) a heavy enemy attack near a graveyard   (D) putting up barbed wire.

REMEMBERING DETAILS

2. The soldier who is most upset by the horses' suffering is

   (A) Paul   (B) Kropp   (C) Katczinsky   (D) Detering.

DRAWING CONCLUSIONS

3. When Paul says that each corpse that was flung up saved one of the men, he means that

   (A) every bullet that hit a corpse was a bullet that couldn't hurt the men   (B) the enemy thought the corpses were newly dead soldiers   (C) the graveyard could only hold so many dead soldiers   (D) the Germans were spooked by the corpses.

THINKING IT OVER

4. If he'd had the chance, Katczinsky would have shot the wounded recruit and ended his suffering. Do you think that would have been the right thing to do? Why or why not?

CHAPTER 5

FINDING THE MAIN IDEA

1. This chapter is mostly about

   (A) the friendship and loyalty the soldiers feel for each other   (B) the trial of Tjaden   (C) Himmelstoss's arrival   (D) roasting a goose.

REMEMBERING DETAILS

2. The one member of the group who has a wife and children to go home to is

   (A) Paul   (B) Kropp   (C) Katczinsky   (D) Tjaden.

DRAWING CONCLUSIONS

3. Tjaden receives a fairly light sentence for insulting Himmelstoss because

   (A) he pays off the lieutenant   (B) he pays off Himmelstoss   (C) Himmelstoss had treated Tjaden badly in the past   (D) the lieutenant likes Tjaden.

USING YOUR REASON

4. Paul and his comrades are glad to see Himmelstoss join their platoon because

(A) they like him   (B) they want him to experience action at the front   (C) they had a bet he would join them   (D) they want him for a leader.

THINKING IT OVER

5. Why do you think Paul suggests that he and Katczinsky share their roasted goose with Tjaden and Kropp? Explain.

CHAPTER 6

FINDING THE MAIN IDEA

1. After the terrible fighting at the front,

(A) the Second Company loses most of its men   (B) the Germans are winning the war   (C) all of Paul's friends are killed   (D) peace is declared.

REMEMBERING DETAILS

2. The troops that attack during the offensive are part of the

(A) British army   (B) Russian army   (C) Italian army
(D) French army.

DRAWING CONCLUSIONS

3. When Paul says that the reinforcements who arrive are almost more trouble than they're worth it's because

(A) they eat too much   (B) they're too inexperienced to help (C) they steal from the other soldiers   (D) they're sympathetic to the enemy.

USING YOUR REASON

4. Paul says the older soldiers have to watch the new recruits in the trench because
(A) they might run away and cause a panic   (B) they talk too loudly   (C) the lieutenant tells them to   (D) they promise the recruits they will.

THINKING IT OVER

5. In this chapter, the author says that the men have become wild beasts. Why do you think they got that way? Explain.

CHAPTER 7

FINDING THE MAIN IDEA

1. This chapter is mostly about

    (A) the Second Company being reorganized   (B) Paul's trip home
    (C) an enemy attack   (D) a visit to a beer garden.

REMEMBERING DETAILS

2. The two comrades who accompany Paul to the train station are

    (A) Kat and Kropp   (B) Tjaden and Müller   (C) Kemmerich and
    Leer   (D) Detering and Müller.

DRAWING CONCLUSIONS

3. Paul doesn't tell his mother how bad it is at the front because

    (A) it isn't really that bad   (B) she won't believe him anyway
    (C) he doesn't want her to worry   (D) he doesn't want to hear her
    cry.

USING YOUR REASON

4. Paul won't tell Kemmerich's mother the truth about how he died
    because

    (A) he knows it will upset her   (B) he is too tired he tell her
    (C) the incident is too painful for Paul to remember
    (D) he doesn't like her very much.

THINKING IT OVER

5. At the end of the chapter, Paul says he should never have come
    home on leave. Why does he feel that way? Explain.

CHAPTER 8

FINDING THE MAIN IDEA

1. While Paul is at the training camp, he gets to

    (A) eat very well   (B) see enemy prisoners up close   (C) meet
    often with his father   (D) learn about new weapons.

REMEMBERING DETAILS

2. Paul's father is worried about

    (A) paying for his wife's operation   (B) his job   (C) his own
    health   (D) Paul's return to the front.

DRAWING CONCLUSIONS

3. At the camp, Paul does not wish for much companionship because
(A) he only feels close to his comrades at the front (B) he doesn't like the camp (C) he knows he'll be leaving soon (D) he likes the Russians better.

USING YOUR REASON

4. Paul has no taste for the potato-cakes his father and sister leave him because
(A) they are rotten (B) he doesn't like potato-cakes (C) he is too upset to have much of an appetite (D) he is saving them for his friends.

THINKING IT OVER

5. Paul says that any non-commissioned officer is more of an enemy to a recruit than the Russians are to the average German soldiers. What do you think he means by that? Explain.

CHAPTER 9

FINDING THE MAIN IDEA

1. This chapter is mostly about
(A) Paul's encounter with a French soldier (B) life in the trenches C) Paul's reunion with his regiment (D) the regiment being sent to Russia.

REMEMBERING DETAILS

2. The French soldier Paul stabs in the trench is
(A) a blacksmith (B) a printer (C) a postman (D) a clerk.

DRAWING CONCLUSIONS

3. Paul hesitates before learning the name of the man he killed because
(A) he doesn't want to touch the dead man (B) the man wouldn't have wanted him to know (C) it is against army rules to learn his name (D) once he learns it, he will always remember killing him.

USING YOUR REASON

4. Paul changes his mind about writing to the dead soldier's family because
(A) he can't write in French (B) he realizes that he is glad he

killed the man (C) it will be difficult to tell them he killed the man (D) he decides that he hated the soldier anyway.

THINKING IT OVER

5. At the end of the chapter, Paul says it was only "nonsense that I talked out there in the shell-hole." He says, "After all, war is war." Do you think he really changes his mind again? Or do you think he only says that to himself so he won't feel guilty about killing the French soldier? Explain.

CHAPTER 10

FINDING THE MAIN IDEA

1. A good title for this chapter might be
   (A) "Wounded in Action" (B) "A Nice Vacation" (C) "Eating and Sleeping Well" (D) "A Catholic Hospital."

REMEMBERING DETAILS

2. Paul's company remains in the abandoned village for nearly
   (A) a month (B) three weeks (C) six months (D) a year.

DRAWING CONCLUSIONS

3. Paul gives the sergeant-major cigars so that he and Kropp can keep together because
   (A) Kropp asks him to (B) they are ordered to (C) they are friends and can look out for each other (D) they promise Kat that they will do so.

USING YOUR REASON

4. Paul insists on being awake while the surgeon operates on him because
   (A) he likes to feel pain (B) he doesn't want the surgeon to amputate his leg (C) the surgeon insists on it (D) they have nothing to put him to sleep with.

THINKING IT OVER

5. Paul says that parting from his friend Albert was very hard. What do you think he said to Albert before they went their separate ways? Write a few sentences that Paul might have said to him.

CHAPTER 11

FINDING THE MAIN IDEA

1. The feeling among the German soldiers in this chapter is that the war is

    (A) now hopelessly lost (B) about to turn in their favor (C) years away from being ended (D) about to be won.

REMEMBERING DETAILS

2. The soldier who was homesick and ran away was

    (A) Paul (B) Kat (C) Tjaden (D) Detering.

DRAWING CONCLUSIONS

3. The soldiers are more upset about being sent back to the front in the Summer of 1918 because

    (A) they don't want to die with rumors of an armistice coming
    (B) it's too hot to fight (C) they are tired of shooting
    (D) they have to fight without guns.

USING YOUR REASON

4. The German surgeons keep sending men back into combat even though they are injured because

    (A) Germany is in desperate need of troops (B) the surgeons are cruel (C) the men want to go back (D) there isn't room in the hospitals.

THINKING IT OVER

5. The orderly at the dressing-station seems puzzled by Paul's reaction to the death of Katczinsky. He even asks Paul if he is related to the dead man. Why do you think he is puzzled? Explain.

CHAPTER 12

FINDING THE MAIN IDEA

1. A good title for this chapter might be

    (A) "Victory" (B) "The End of Everything" (C) "Defeat"
    (D) "Peace."

REMEMBERING DETAILS

2. Paul gets 14 days rest because

    (A) he asks for it (B) he is wounded badly (C) he swallows a bit of gas (D) his mother dies.

USING YOUR REASON

3. Paul holds out some hope that he will feel differently about life when he returns home because

    (A) he needs something to live for (B) he does not feel that badly (C) he's eager to get back to his job (D) he knows everything at home is fine.

THINKING IT OVER

4. Before Paul is actually killed, one could say he is already "dead inside." Find some evidence in the last chapter to support that statement. Explain.